DENIM DIARIES 3:

QUEEN OF THE YARD

DENIM DIARIES 3:

QUEEN OF THE YARD

DARRIEN LEE

www.urbanbooks.com

Urban Books
1199 Straight Path
West Babylon, NY 11704

ISBN-13: 978-1-933967-77-6
ISBN-10: 1-933967-77-3

First Printing July 2009
Printed in the United States of America

10   9   8   7   6   5   4

Distributed by Kensington Publishing Corp.
Submit Wholesale Orders to:
Kensington Publishing Corp.
C/O Penguin Group (USA) Inc.
Attention: Order Processing
405 Murray Hill Parkway
East Rutherford, NJ 07073-2316
Phone: 1-800-526-0275
Fax: 1-800-227-9604

Prologue

The night was unusually warm and you could smell the threat of rain in the air, but for Jasmine Baxter, known by her friends as Jazz, the night was perfect. She laughed as the members of B.G.R. kicked and beat the two newest members of their group. They were being jumped in and it was brutal. One girl was a freshman and the other was a sophomore at Langley High. Jazz's older sister, Patience, stood in the shadows of the vacant warehouse and watched as the beatings finally came to an end as quickly as they started. Jazz laughed out loud and motioned for her sister to join them. When Patience walked over to the group she helped both of the girls off the ground. What happened next had become somewhat of a ritual with Patience. She smiled at the two girls and then punched them square in the jaw, knocking them onto the ground. Both girls grimaced in pain as they lay on the ground. Patience smiled and helped the two girls up after which she hugged them and then said, "Now you're B.G.R."

Patience was the head of a local high school girl's clan called B.G.R., which was the abbreviation for *brown girls rule*. Brianna Baxter was her real name and she had obtained the nickname Patience because she never rushed into anything without carefully thinking about it from all angles. Therefore, she was tagged with the alias Patience. Scotland Heights, better known as the Yard, was their territory. It was a neighborhood known for its high crime, gang activity, and low-income status. Most of the news that came from this area was of shootings, robberies, and drug deals. Few success stories came out of their area and those that did never made it into the news.

Patience joined B.G.R when she was only fourteen years old because it allowed her to have a sense of security when she was on the streets in a neighborhood infested by drugs and crime. She'd always been tall for her age, giving others the perception that she was much older. Over the years, she rose from a neophyte to the head of the group, gaining a lot of respect along the way. Even her younger sister, Jazz, had followed in her footsteps by joining the group who had become feared by some and respected by others. Jazz was next in line to take over B.G.R. in a couple of months when Patience graduated from high school. At that point she would be officially an O.G., original gangster.

"Dang, Patience!" Jazz yelled before laughing. "You're vicious!"

All the other members clapped and started celebrating among themselves while Jazz and Patience found a seat on the hood of Patience's car.

"I'm not vicious, Jazz, and this is getting old."

"No, you're getting old. This is tradition," her sister reminded her.

Patience looked over at her sister and asked, "What's the point of beating girls to join up with us?"

"Duh! To make sure they got what it takes to be in B.G.R. We're challenged every day around here on the Yard. Scotland Heights is our hood and we have to look out for each other," Jazz reminded her.

Patience and Jazz looked over at the group of girls as they clapped and danced to the music coming from one of the car stereos. The initiation celebration had kicked off with plenty of music, food, and laughter. Some were smoking cigarettes while others passed forty-ounce bottles of beer around. While none of them was old enough to drink there never was a shortage of the brown brew. All of them knew someone who was old enough and willing to buy the alcohol and cigarettes for them for a small price, of course.

"I'm not feeling the direction B.G.R. is going in and before I leave, there are some changes that I want to see done."

"What are you talking about? This is the way things have been done for ten years."

She turned to Jazz and then pointed to the crowd. "Look at them. Almost everyone here has some type of scar on their body or a juvie charge."

"We don't. We've never seen the inside of juvenile court," Jazz reminded her.

"I know, but it's because we've been blessed and we know better. Some of the girls think having a juvenile record is some type of badge of honor."

"Patience, we do what we have to do to survive. Scotland Heights is not exactly the land of opportunity, which means some of the girls have to take what they can."

"At what cost, Jazz?" Patience asked. "I don't

want to end up behind bars before I can get out here and I don't want to see you locked up, either. It will kill Momma."

Irritated, Jazz said, "Everybody's not like you! You're one of the lucky ones, sis. You got a full college scholarship and that's your ticket out."

"I worked hard for my scholarship and it's possible for you and anyone else up here on the Yard to do the same thing."

"Opportunity hasn't knocked on too many doors up here," Jazz pointed out. "You have to admit that and if B.G.R. stops being who they are, those other gangs will eat us alive."

"I'm not saying B.G.R can't defend themselves. I'm talking about the other stuff. You know, being bag chicks for drug dealers, fighting and other stuff. Bullets don't have eyes and I don't want one hitting any of us. I thought you would've learned by what happened to Daddy and Ryan."

Jazz sat there in deep thought for a moment as visions of her lost loved ones cycled through her head. Talking about their father and brother was never easy for either one of them and the grief was still fresh. Their brother, Ryan, was a police officer who was killed during a routine traffic stop. He'd only been on the job for six months when his life ended at the tender age of twenty-two. The killer or killers were never caught.

Their father's death resulted when he found himself caught in the middle of a robbery at a neighborhood store where he had stopped on his way home. The store clerk pulled out a gun and exchanged gunfire with the robber. When it was all over it was their father who was killed by a stray bullet as he crouched down for cover in the back of the store.

"Why you got to bring up Daddy and Ryan?"

"How else can I make you to understand where I'm coming from?" Patience asked.

Patience and Jazz both picked up their father's genes, who was of Hawaiian decent. They both had his slanted dark eyes and thick, wavy hair. They had their mother's African-American physique, which consisted of a curvaceous body and a cinnamon complexion. Patience, however, was blessed with long, shapely legs and stood at six feet tall. Her hair was dark auburn and hung midway down her back. However, Jazz stood only about five feet five inches tall. She possessed shoulder-length reddish-brown hair, a hair color she'd inherited from their maternal grandmother.

Their parents met while in college and it was

love at first sight. Scotland Heights was a community with mixed ethnicities and, contrary to belief, not everyone there was low income. Some people loved the area for its historic appeal. Their father was a proud man and had worked as an electrician with the local power company. He made a lucrative income for his family and was a great father and husband. Their mother, Selena, was a paralegal and at one time thought about going to law school but changed her mind after the death of her husband.

"I know where you're coming from, sis, but I don't like talking about Daddy and Ryan," Jazz admitted.

Patience frowned. "So you just want to forget about them and block them out of your mind?"

"No, I'll never forget them but it still hurts to actually talk about them."

Jazz was only ten years old when their father died and twelve years old when Ryan was killed. While it seemed like it was a lifetime ago, the memories were still fresh on both of their minds. They were both daddy's girls and losing a parent is never easy. When they lost their brother, who had stepped up as a father figure, the girls fell apart emotionally. While they loved their mother dearly, they became numb to violence on the streets.

"I'm sorry, Jazz."

"Don't be. I'm cool."

Jazz was trying to be tough and not let her soft side come out, but if there was anyone she could show her soft side to, it was her sister. She understood her better than anyone. The mood had become solemn and Patience wanted desperately to liven things up.

"If you hit the books a little harder maybe you can join me."

"And leave all of this?" she joked.

Patience shoved Jazz playfully and said, "You know what I mean."

"I'm just kidding with you, but seriously, if I leave, Momma will be here all alone," Jazz replied.

"If something bad happened to us, Momma would still be alone. Her being alone because we're in college is a lot better than her being alone because we're in the grave."

"You have a point when you look at it that way."

Patience slid off the hood of her car and said, "I still plan to make some changes with B.G.R. before I leave for college."

"It's one thing to tell me, but you bet not let the others hear you talking about changing B.G.R. because they'll go ballistic."

"Well, they can go to hell because I'm running B.G.R. and nobody else."

Jazz snapped her fingers and said, "That I can't argue with."

Now that the jump in was over, Jazz slid off the hood of the car and made the announcement for everyone to meet in the city park to celebrate the initiation with hot wings and fries.

Patience climbed behind the wheel of her car, as Jazz climbed into the passenger seat.

"I think I'm going to call it a night, Jazz," Patience replied with less enthusiasm. "You and the girls go on to the park and kick it. I'm going home."

"Come on, Patience."

"No, I'll pass on this one. Besides, I have a test I need to study for."

Concerned over Patience's odd behavior, Jazz looked at her and asked, "What's happening to you? First you want to shake up B.G.R. and now you don't even want to hang with us. You've never missed a jumping in celebration and you and I both know that you ace all your tests."

Patience pulled out of the warehouse district and said, "Well, there's a first for everything and regardless of what you think, I never take a test without studying for it."

"What's really going on, Patience? It can't just be this thing with B.G.R."

"I have a lot of stuff on my mind. That's all," she revealed.

Jazz smiled and then asked, "Are you pregnant or something?"

Patience looked over at Jazz in disbelief. "Where did that come from?"

"I was just wondering. You're so secretive about your personal life. You used to tell me everything. Now I don't even know if there's a man in your life."

Patience shook her head and said, "I'm not pregnant, Jazz, so relax. I don't know why your mind always goes there anyway."

"That answers one of my questions. So, are you seeing anybody?" Jazz asked.

"Maybe. You know I don't like to kiss and tell. How did we get on that subject anyway?"

Jazz laughed. She was always trying to find out if her sister was dating because she was nosy like that.

"Why does it matter if I'm seeing someone?" Patience asked.

"I'm just curious."

"Stop worrying about my love life. Cool?"

"Whatever you say, sis."

Patience pulled up to a red light and turned to her sister. "Why you all up in my business, let's talk about you."

"Oh, here we go," Jazz answered as she rolled her eyes.

"No, Jazz, your grades are jacked up and you pick the worst guys to hang out with. Is it wrong for me to say anything?"

"As far as Red Rum, so what if I like my men a little rough around the edges?" Jazz asked. "He's no different than us."

"Red Rum is nothing like us. He's a thug and so are the guys he hangs with."

"Whatever," she mumbled.

"Listen to me! Things are more dangerous now! B.G.R. is not like it was when I joined. The girls are getting more brazen and violent. That's not what I signed up for and neither did you and you know it."

"The change is the signs of the times," Jazz pointed out. "Life is hard in the Yard and if you keep talking about changing B.G.R. I don't know what the girls will do."

The light turned green and Patience continued down the street.

"I don't care what they think."

Jazz sat next to her sister in silence for a few minutes.

"I understand about college, but changing B.G.R. on your way out is not going to go over well with the sisterhood."

Patience laughed.

"Whether they like it or not, they have to follow my orders."

"Maybe," Jazz replied.

"If they don't, there will be hell to pay and you know it."

"Like I said, maybe," Jazz replied.

There was another moment of silence between the two until Jazz finally spoke up.

"I want you to know that if you do this, those girls won't have an ounce of respect for me when I take over."

"Yes they will."

"I'm not like you. I mean, I can hold my own but you're a legend in B.G.R. and I've seen you in action, remember? You're hard-core."

Patience let out a loud sigh. "That was a long time ago. Besides, once you take over as queen of the Yard, your respect has already been established."

Patience had worked her way up through the ranks to become head of the gang. It was a hard-fought battle but she had earned the honor and gained the reputation among rival gangs of being ruthless and unforgiving.

"Have you forgotten where you come from? You can't outrun your reputation."

Patience laughed. "I've never done anything that didn't need to be done. If you heard anything different, it's a lie."

Now it was Jasmine's turn to laugh.

"I'm your sister, remember? I know for a fact that you're a badass."

Patience turned away from her sister so she couldn't see her smile.

"I don't care how much you try to clean it up. People fear you for a reason."

"It's a curse and an honor," Patience revealed. "I'm not proud of some of the things I've done but I have no regrets," she announced as she adjusted the volume on the CD player.

Just then, a car pulled out in front of them, blocking their path. Patience slammed on the brakes and watched as three guys jumped out of the car with bandannas over their faces.

"What is this?" Jazz asked nervously.

"Be cool," Patience instructed her as she slowly slid her hands between the seats. She gripped the cold metal and waited. The smell of burnt rubber from the screeching tires stung their nostrils as they sat in the car and waited.

"Get out of the car!" one of the men instructed them as he stood in front of the car with his gun held gangster style.

Jazz looked down at Patience's hand and knew exactly what she was doing.

"Patience?" Jazz called out to her.

"Don't worry, Jazz. I got this," Patience replied. "I'm not going to let anything happen to you."

Chapter One

"That was foul, Red Rum!" Patience yelled at Jazz's boyfriend as she shoved him in the chest. "I could've killed you!"

Red Rum, which is *murder* spelled backward, laughed and then kissed Jazz on the lips. "Come on, Patience, you know I was just having a little fun with you."

Angry, Patience turned to Jazz and asked, "Did you know it was him?"

Jazz could see that her sister was furious. She reluctantly replied, "Not at first but once he started yelling I did."

Patience cursed all of them out then climbed back into her car. She turned on the ignition and sat there for a second, rethinking just how close she came to firing her gun.

"Where are you going?" Jazz asked as she approached Patience's car.

"I told you I was going home. This is exactly the kind of mess I was talking about in the car! These fools up here on the Yard play too much!"

"It was a joke, Patience," Jazz pleaded.

"A joke? That kind of joke will get somebody killed! Do you have any idea what could've jumped off?"

"Calm down! Nothing happened! Dang!" Jazz yelled.

Jazz could feel the heat from her sister's anger and see the fury in her eyes.

"You know what? I'm out of here!" Patience yelled.

"So you're just going to leave me here?" Jazz asked.

She put the car in drive and said, "Get Red Rum to take you. I'm out!"

Jazz stood and watched in disbelief as Patience squealed her tires as she drove away.

"Dang, babe, Patience is pissed, huh?" Red Rum asked as he grabbed her around the waist and pulled her against his chest.

"Yeah, she's a little upset."

He put his arm around her shoulders and walked her over to the car. "Don't worry about Patience. She'll be all right after she cools off."

"I hope you're right," she replied as she looked down the street in the direction her sister had driven. "Listen, can you guys take me to the Wing Depot? I have to pick up some hot wings for B.G.R's jumping-in celebration in the park. You guys can come if you want to."

Red Rum opened the car door for Jasmine so she could climb into backseat of the eighty-six Monte Carlo he was riding in.

"All you had to do was say hot wings, baby, and we're there. Let's roll."

Denim had been driving around Scotland Heights for some time. After hearing the girls in the deli talking about Patience, she figured she owed it to Patience to let her know. She didn't know her address but she knew the vicinity. At that moment her cell phone rang.

"Hello?"

"Denim, Dré's been trying to get in touch with you. He said your cell is going into your voice mail."

"My cell must be out of area," she replied.

DeMario was not only one of her closest friends and like a brother to her. He was also the best friend of her boyfriend, André Patterson.

"Where are you?" DeMario asked.

"Don't blow a gasket or tell Dré but I'm in Scotland Heights."

"Scotland Heights?" DeMario asked curiously. "What the hell are you doing in the Yard?"

"It's a long story, DeMario. I can't talk now, but I'll tell you later."

He laughed. "You're not going to get rid of me that easy. Now tell why you're in Scotland Heights?"

"If you must know, I'm looking for Patience," she revealed.

"Patience?" he asked. "Have you lost your mind?"

"Look, I can take care of myself," she assured him.

"Not in the Yard, you can't. Where are you?" he asked, somewhat irritated.

Denim looked around and said, "I'm not really sure. I see a Publix, a check-cashing store, a liquor store, and a Sonic. There's a Taco Bell and a car wash across the street."

"I know where you are. I just left my grandmother's house. She lives a couple of miles from there. Pull into the Taco Bell and I'll meet you there in five minutes," he instructed her. "Make sure your doors are locked and don't get out of your car."

Just then, Denim noticed Patience pulling into the Sonic drive-in.

"DeMario, meet me at the Sonic instead. I just saw Patience pull in."

"I'm on my way. Don't do anything stupid, Denim!" DeMario yelled into the telephone before hanging up.

Denim quickly turned her vehicle around and also pulled into the fast-food restaurant. As she exited her car against DeMario's wishes and walked over to Patience, she remembered her first encounter with her. Well, it was more than an encounter. Patience had actually saved her from getting jumped by three bullies in the restroom and every since then she felt that she owed her a favor. Now was her chance to wipe the slate clean.

Patience sat at the table alone, neatly dressed in some form-fitting Apple Bottom jeans with a T-shirt knotted in the back. Her midsection was exposed, revealing an earring that dangled from her navel.

She had just ordered her food and when she looked up, she found Denim standing across from her looking somewhat perplexed.

"Aren't you lost, Mitchell?"

"No, I know exactly where I am. I came up here to find you. Do you mind if I sit down?" Denim asked.

Patience laughed and then shook her head in disbelief. "Help yourself. It's a public place."

Denim looked around at all the other patrons and noticed that people was staring at her. She was an unfamiliar face in a tight-knit community where most everyone knew each other, even those who were considered rivals. Territory meant everything to them and having an outsider hanging around at a local hangout raised curiosity among the teens.

Denim sat down across from Patience and said, "Thanks."

"You want something to eat?" Patience asked as she pointed to the menu.

"Oh, no, I'm fine."

The waitress brought Patience her order of popcorn chicken, fries, and a cherry limeade.

"That will be six dollars and seventy-five cents,"

the waitress told Patience. She pulled out a ten and said, "Keep the change."

The waitress smiled and said, "Thanks."

Once the waitress was gone, Patience immediately took a sip of her drink. She pointed at her food and asked, "Are you sure you don't want anything? I don't mind sharing."

Denim smiled. She couldn't help but smell the aroma of chicken, burgers, and fries in the air. Her stomach growled in response even though she'd recently eaten.

"No, I'm fine, really."

"Okay, Mitchell, why are you here? This is not exactly your side of town," Patience pointed out.

Before Denim could answer a young man dressed in a Walter Payton Chicago Bears throw-back jersey walked over and sat down next to Patience. With several gold chains and what looked like a diamond-stud earring in his ear, he nodded in Denim's direction and asked, "Hey, Patience. Who's your friend?"

"Get lost, Lionel," Patience replied. "She's not into guys like you."

He frowned and said, "What you saying? She thinks she's better than me?"

Denim stood up to defend herself. "No, I don't think—"

"Sit down, Mitchell," Patience calmly instructed her.

"Then what's up?" Lionel yelled, interrupting Patience.

Patience laughed.

"Lionel, you need to chill. Mitchell's cool. I was just messing with you, but seriously, she don't date thugs."

"You know I go by L. J. and I'm not a thug," he announced.

"Then what are you, Lionel?" Patience asked as she pointed at his midsection. "I see you're still packing that nine millimeter in your waistband, so you tell me. Are you a thug or aren't you?"

He laughed. "I am what I am," he acknowledged.

"Then I rest my case. Mitchell only dates athletes and you definitely don't fit in that category."

Lionel laughed and reached over and grabbed a French fry off her tray.

"You're a trip, Patience."

"Hey!" Patience yelled as she smacked his hand.

Denim watched as Lionel rejoined his friends. She turned her attention back to Patience and asked, "Was he really carrying a gun?"

Patience dipped a piece of chicken in her honey mustard and said, "Up here on the Yard, everybody carries a gun. I thought you knew, but then again you wouldn't know anything about that, would you?"

Denim stared at Patience for a moment and then said, "I know life can be hard on some people but you'll be headed off the college soon, right?" she asked.

Patience snapped at Denim and said, "This is not exactly the neighborhood of opportunity, but it's my hood so don't disrespect it."

"I don't mean to disrespect you. All I'm saying is that people who live here don't have to become a product of their environment."

Patience frowned. She was irritated by Denim's remarks but she had to admit there was some truth to what she was saying.

"Are you trying to judge me, Mitchell?"

"You're taking what I said the wrong way."

"Then what are you trying to say?" Patience asked.

"One thing I didn't come up here to do was piss you off.," Denim explained. "Maybe I should just leave."

When Denim tried to get up Patience grabbed her wrist.

"I'm not pissed off yet but you're about to take me there. Sit down and tell me why you're here."

Denim eased back into her seat and softly said, "I came up her because I overheard some girls talking about taking you out."

While it wasn't news or the first time rivals had wanted to take her out, this was the first time the news had come from the outside and she had to admit that she was a little bit curious about the information. Retaliation was something gang members had to expect when living the lifestyle, therefore Denim's news wasn't a shock to her.

"So, who were these girls?"

Denim hesitated and then revealed the bombshell.

"I don't know their names but they were pissed and they're in B.G.R."

Patience was used to having enemies but not in her own crew. It was unthinkable and unheard of in the history of B.G.R.

"You're crazy! It can't be any of my girls."

"I'm not crazy and I know those girls are a part of B.G.R."

Patience leaned back in her seat and folded her arms defensively.

"Then explain to me why people from my own crew would want to take me out?"

"I can't answer that because I didn't hear their whole conversation," Denim admitted.

"This sounds like some bull, Mitchell."

Patience was having a hard time accepting a coup in her crew and Denim didn't expect her to react in anger. She expected her to be thankful, not defensive, so she decided it was best that she quit while she was ahead.

"I just thought you should know what was going on behind your back."

"Well, thanks for nothing!" Patience yelled, drawing attention in their direction.

Lionel walked back over to the table and asked, "Is everything cool?"

Patience shook her head and said, "Yeah, everything's good."

"Are you sure?" he asked as he stared down at Denim.

"Yeah, I'm sure, L. J."

He put a toothpick in his mouth and said, "All right, but call me if you need me."

Patience nodded in agreement as Lionel made his way back over to his table. After he was gone Patience gave Denim a look that could melt steel.

"Do you have any idea what you've done?" Patience whispered.

Naive to what Patience was trying to explain, Denim responded, "I thought what I was doing was a good thing by telling you, but I see I made a mistake. Just forget I was ever here."

Denim hurried toward her car but Patience called out to her.

"Wait, Mitchell!"

She stopped and slowly turned around to face Patience, who motioned for Denim to come back and sit down. She watched Patience as she put her hands over her face in deep thought as she wondered who and why her own would turn against her. She had to absorb what she just heard and decide how she was going to handle the information. The suspense was killing Denim as she waited in silence to see what she was going to say or do next.

"Look, you're going to have to give me a minute. It's not everyday that I find out that my crew has some traitors."

"I understand," Denim responded softly.

Patience took a sip of her cherry limeade to moisten her dry throat. One thing she knew she had to do was give Denim credit for coming to

Scotland Heights. It wasn't a neighborhood you hung out in unless you lived there or were looking for trouble and Denim didn't fit in either category. She could've easily waited to tell her this information at school.

"Okay, I need details. When and where did you hear this conversation?"

"It was Martelli's deli near the hospital this afternoon," Denim revealed.

"I'm getting ready to find out who the bitches are," Patience replied. "Let's go."

"What do you mean, let's go?" Denim asked in a high-pitched voice. "I hope you don't expect me to go with you to confront those girls."

Patience stood and said, "All you have to do is get in your car and follow me. When we get there you let me know if you recognize any of the voices as I talk to them."

Denim's jaw dropped in disbelief. The last thing she wanted to do was come face-to-face with B.G.R. on their turf. About that time, DeMario pulled up and quickly exited the vehicle. He made his way over to where Denim and Patience were standing and twirled his car keys on his finger.

Patience laughed out loud and said, "Well, here come the cavalry."

Denim looked over at him and noticed the frustrated look on his face.

"What's up, Patience?"

"Hey, DeMario. I guess you came over here to make sure Mitchell was still in one piece, huh?"

"Something like that," he replied before turning to face his friend. "Denim, I thought I told you to wait for me."

"You took too long."

"Well, I'm here now and you need to get back to Langley Hills," he announced as he nudged her toward the parking lot. "The Yard is no place for you."

Patience stepped in between the pair.

"Not so fast, DeMario. Denim just told me some important information and we were just about to go check it out."

"What could be so important that you need Denim?"

Before Patience could answer Denim quickly filled DeMario in on the conversation she overheard. Once she finished he shook his head in disbelief.

"Okay, you've warned Patience; now the rest has nothing to do with you. Let's go."

"Wait a second," Patience requested. "Denim didn't have to risk her life by coming up here."

"I know she didn't, but you're going to have to get to the truth without her. You and I both know she's out of her element up here."

"Can I say something?" Denim asked, trying to get a word in between Patience and DeMario.

Ignoring her, Patience put her hand on DeMario's shoulder.

"Relax, bro. All she has to do is listen to their voices and point them out to me and I'll take it from there."

"No, I can't let her get involved."

"Excuse me, I'm standing right here," Denim announced as she waved her hands in their faces to try and get their attention. Unfortunately, they still ignored her and continued their conversation.

Patience knew the friendship between Denim and DeMario was like a sibling bond and she had to respect his concern for her safety.

"Chill, DeMario. You know I wouldn't put Mitchell out like that. All she has to do is follow my lead. You're welcome to come along if you want to."

"Is anybody listening to me?" Denim yelled.

"No!" Patience and DeMario yelled in unison.

Denim put her hands on her hips in disbelief.

Here they were talking about her like she wasn't even there. She wasn't a child and while she was a little nervous being in Scotland Heights, she felt like she needed to finish what she started even though it might put her in danger.

"Wait a minute, DeMario. I think I do want to help Patience after all."

DeMario adjusted his baseball cap. "You think?"

"She helped me that time when Zeta and her girls challenged me. It's only fair that I do the same for her. Zeta and her girls could've really hurt me that day in the restroom but they didn't, all because Patience stepped in."

DeMario understood that some female fights could be just as brutal as male brawls and had Patience not stepped in and helped Denim, Zeta and her friends could've really hurt her.

"DeMario, I need her," Patience pleaded with him. "Nobody's going to mess with Denim up here. She'll be with me and I'm queen of the Yard. You know me. My word is golden, I promise."

DeMario wasn't totally convinced she would be able to keep Denim safe.

"I know you're queen of the Yard, but B.G.R. is not the only gang in Scotland Heights and I don't want Denim mixed up in any drama, especially drama between you and your girls."

"It's okay, DeMario. I'll be fine," Denim assured him.

"Maybe so, but it's getting late. I don't feel like tonight is a good night to front anybody without getting more info," DeMario suggested.

Before DeMario could respond, Patience said, "You know what, you're right, DeMario. I need to give this more thought. You've given me more than enough to work with. Don't worry about me because I definitely plan on following up on what I can tonight."

Denim held her fist out to Patience and said, "I'm sorry I won't be able to go with you."

"It's okay, Mitchell," Patience replied as she bumped her fist against Denim's to assure her their relationship was still cool.

"I guess I'll see you at school, huh?" Denim asked.

"No doubt," Patience answered. "And don't beat yourself up about not being able to go with me. I'll get to the bottom of it one way or another."

Denim smiled as she backed away from Patience. "I'll try not to. Good-bye."

As Denim walked to her car she had a slight

sense of accomplishment in warning Patience but deep down inside she still felt like she was leaving something undone. Yes, she'd given Patience somewhere to start in her investigation but there was still so much unknown. Most importantly, who was involved and why they wanted to take her out. Hopefully, the answers would come to her sooner rather than later.

"I'll see you around, DeMario," Patience yelled out to him as he opened the door to his car.

"Stay safe," he yelled back before he climbed inside his car and trailed Denim down the street and out of sight.

On the way home Patience decided to take a detour and drive by the city park after all to see if she could get any idea of who the traitors were. The answer to why, she would beat out of them after she identified them. To her knowledge, she'd never done anything to make her girls want to betray her, but some wounds cut deep and just maybe she had pushed someone to the point of retaliation.

As Patience pulled into the park she noticed a very familiar physique. It was a physique that mirrored her own so there was no mistaking who it was.

"Momma, what are you doing here?" she mumbled to herself.

Patience watched as her mother hugged and kissed a man before climbing inside his car. They'd obviously been walking together in the park and now they were leaving. The car backed out of the parking space and slowly made its way toward the exit. Patience quickly pulled onto a side street and turned off her headlights. She held her breath as she waited for the car to make its way in her direction. Her mother hadn't dated that she knew of since their father died. Now she couldn't be so sure.

Patience slumped down in the seat of her car as the vehicle passed directly in front of her, confirming that it was in fact her mother in the car with a strange man. She got a good look at him as well and quickly jotted down the license plate. Once they had exited the park, she sat up and stared at the license plate number on the paper. Now she wondered why her mother hadn't told her or Jazz about her new love interest. She decided not to tell Jazz until she had more information so she shook the thoughts out of her mind before putting the license plate number into her glove compartment.

Minutes later she pulled her car into a parking space in the section of the park where B.G.R. members had gathered. Patience exited the vehicle and walked toward the group. As she got closer she could see that the party had picked up right where it left off. She could smell cigarette smoke, weed, and the aroma of hot wings in the air and the sounds of rapper Lil' Wayne blasting from one of the car stereos. It was an unusually humid night and as she moved even closer she could hear a few of the girls cussing like sailors as they sat around on picnic tables. That's when she got her mind back on track to the reason she was there, which was to identify the traitors.

Upon reaching the group she observed how Jazz, B.G.R. members along with Red Rum and his crew were partying. It was as if they didn't have a care in the world and that life as they knew it was eternal and spectacular.

"Hey, sis!" Jazz greeted her excitedly and she jumped off the picnic table. "I thought you weren't coming. What changed your mind?"

"Let's just say I had a change of heart," she replied as she reached into one of the cardboard boxes and pulled out a hot wing. Before taking a bite she looked at all twenty girls and carefully and discreetly studied them. They seemed so happy and proud to be there as a group and all of them appeared to be happy that she had joined them after all as they flashed their B.G.R. sign to her with huge smiles on their faces.

"Yo, Patience. Are you still mad at me?" Red Rum asked as he tugged on his oversized jeans while walking in her direction.

She put her hand up to his face and said, "Don't even talk to me. You were wrong and you know it."

"Come on, Patience," he begged as he tried to hug her. "Don't be like that. You know I'm your boy."

Patience tried to push him away but he had her in a bear hug.

"No, you're not, now get off me!"

He laughed and gave her a kiss on the cheek.

"I had to make sure you were up on your game," he explained as he released her. "You know you can't get lazy around here."

"I'm up on my game, all right," she replied as she rubbed the spot on her cheek where he had kissed her. "I'm so up on my game that I almost killed you, you fool!"

"Not in this lifetime, sweetheart," he replied. "You're good, but you're not that good."

She winked at him and said, "Don't let the smooth taste fool you."

Patience's comment was taken from an infamous beer commercial recited by actor Billy Dee Williams. Her mother used the line all the time so one day she decided to ask her what it meant, which was don't be fooled by the softness because it was bolder than it appeared. She'd been using it ever since.

Red Rum smiled, showing her his gold teeth. "I respect that. You know you're all right with me any day."

She tossed the chicken bone into the garbage can without thanking him for his compliment.

"I have some business to discuss with my girls so if you don't mind . . ."

"You don't have to tell me but once," Red Rum replied before motioning for his boys to follow him. Before walking away, Red Rum pulled Jazz into his arms and gave her a huge kiss on the lips. Jazz happily returned the kiss before slowly releasing him.

"Later, baby," she said softly to him as he walked away.

Once they were gone, Patience turned back to her girls. This was going to be a delicate matter to resolve. She didn't want to accuse the wrong girls but she did want the culprits revealed as quickly as possible, so having Denim ID the voices was going to be the best thing to do.

Patience pulled Jazz over to the side so they could talk in private.

"Jazz, I don't want B.G.R. to be associated with Red Rum and his boys, so do me a favor and stop bringing him around so much."

Jazz folded her arms and rolled her eyes. "Oh, here we go again."

"They're criminals, Jazz, and if the police start associating you or B.G.R. with them, the police are going to put two and two together and think we're just like them."

"Correct me if I'm wrong, but B.G.R. is not completely innocent either."

"Compared to them? Jazz, please! B.G.R. girls are nowhere close to being like them and you know it, so don't get it twisted."

"Illegal is illegal," Jazz announced. "I can't count how many times we could've been put in juvenile hall for some of the stuff we've done."

"That's where you're wrong, baby sis. We were careful but if you keep hanging around Red Rum, your luck is going to run out."

Jazz was angry now. Discussing Red Rum had always been a sensitive subject between the sisters. Jazz was well aware that he dabbled in a few illegal activities but he had a good heart and he loved her and she loved him. Patience would just have to get over it because she wasn't going to continue to let her dog him. Yes, he was a little rough around the edges but who wasn't? He was her man and she didn't like her talking down about him.

"My luck is just fine, thank you!"

"You need to drop the attitude because you know I'm right. He's not good for you."

Jazz rolled her eyes again.

Patience laughed.

"I see you rolling your eyes at me, but that's cool. You're my sister and I love you. That's all that really matters."

Patience held her fist out to Jazz as a peace offering to her sister. Jazz bumped her fist against her big sister's and jokingly asked, "Can't we all just get along?"

The two sisters laughed together and then hugged each other. Upon releasing her sister, Jazz asked, "Seriously, Patience, I don't want to argue about Red Rum anymore. Can't you just let me do my thang? I know what I'm doing."

Patience put her arm around her sister's shoulder and said, "I'm sorry to disappoint you, but no. He's going to end up in jail or dead and I don't want you anywhere near him when it happens, now I'm through talking about him."

"Patience," Jazz pleaded.

She put her finger in Jazz's face and said, "I said no! Now come on, I have some unpleasant business to take care of."

"What kind of business?" Jazz asked. She didn't know exactly what her sister was going to do but whatever it was she knew by the stern look on her face it was going to have a huge impact on B.G.R. Anxious to hear what she was going to say, she quickly followed her sister and rejoined the group. Then, in tomboy fashion, Patience put her fingers in her mouth and let out a loud whistle to get everyone's attention. Once everyone had settled down and the music was turned down, all eyes were on her.

"What I'm about to say will probably come as a shock to you guys, but as queen of the Yard I have to follow my heart and my mind and do what I know is best for us as a crew. With that said, I wanted to let you guys know that I've decided that tonight will be our last initiation and once the youngest members graduate from high school, it's over."

There were immediate whispers from the girls. Patience expected some opposition and grumbling from the group but if anyone wanted to take it to the next level she was prepared for that as well. She was hoping that her announcement might bring the traitors out into the open. Surely whoever they were, they would be the main ones against her making such a drastic change for B.G.R.

"What do you mean when you say it's over?" Jazz asked. She was not only curious herself but she knew the crew was confused by Patience's announcement.

"It means exactly what I said. Over means over, which means I'm dissolving B.G.R. once and for all."

By the looks on the crew members' faces, it was obvious that they were in shock. B.G.R. has been like a family to some of the girls and dissolving it could be disastrous, especially once rival gangs found out they were on their own.

"That's suicide for us if you do that, sis."

Patience turned to her sister and gave her the eye. It wasn't protocol for crew members to question the head of a gang even if she was her sister. It didn't help that Jazz was doing it in front of the crew so at this moment she wasn't her sister. She was just a member of her crew.

All eyes were on Patience. No one knew exactly why she was closing down B.G.R. The reasoning behind her decision might eventually come out in the open but if it didn't, the crew normally would have to accept it as a direct order from the queen of the Yard, but everything about this night was different and she did something totally out of the norm.

"So does anybody have anything they want to say?" she asked.

The crew members looked around at each other and waited for someone else to respond. None of them wanted to put their neck out on the line.

"Nobody has anything to say because now is the time," Patience revealed. "It's now or never."

Still no response. She really didn't expect anyone to confront her but there was always a first. This news was big and it was going to affect the lives of all of them, especially Jazz, since she was still going to be around. She had a feeling that some of the crew might put pressure on her to keep B.G.R. going just as soon as Patience was off to college. In fact, deep down inside, she was thinking about doing that very thing. Jazz wasn't ready to let go of B.G.R., but if she defied Patience's order, it would go against years of B.G.R. history.

"Okay, if nobody has any questions I want to welcome our newest and last members of B.G.R. and I'm sure—"

"I have a question," one of the crew members said as she interrupted Patience and took a puff of her cigarette.

Patience eyed the crew member who had been in B.G.R. for two years. Her name was Desireé and she had no problem looking Patience in the eyes. Could she be one of the girls Denim overheard or was she just a curious crew member looking for answers?

"What's your question?" Patience asked.

Desireé jumped down off the picnic table and walked closer to Patience. She stopped a few feet away from her and then put her cigarette out in the dirt.

"You're leaving for college after graduation, right?" Desireé asked.

"That's no secret," Patience replied.

"Then why the drama?" She pointed over to Jazz and said, "Jazz has already been established as the next queen of the Yard. Why do you want to break up our family?"

Patience walked over to Desireé until they were face-to-face. She didn't blink and neither did Desireé. The other crew members looked on nervously, not sure what would happen next. You could cut the tension with a knife. Jazz realized that if something jumped off between the two she would have to make sure it was a fair fight.

Patience put her hands on her hips and said, "B.G.R. is out of control. I don't like Red Rum and his boys hanging around and don't think I don't know that some of you are making money by being errand girls for them. They're going to get you locked up or killed."

"Wait a minute, Patience," Jazz interrupted.

"Stay out of this, Jazz."

"So what if we want to make a little money with Red Rum and his crew?" Desireé asked.

A groaning noise radiated from the group. Desireé may not have realized it or she didn't care that she was about to get in over head.

She frowned and then looked Patience up and down. "We have plans for B.G.R. after you leave. I think it's best that you—"

Before Desireé could finish her sentence, Patience

grabbed her by the neck. Her hands were fast, so fast that it caught the crew off guard.

"Desireé, it's one thing to ask me a question. It's another thing to disrespect me in the process. You need to stop while you're ahead."

The rest of the crew immediately circled the two girls, not knowing exactly what to do next.

Jazz looked up at her sister and softly said, "Let her go, Patience. We're not supposed to fight with each other."

Patience released her grip on Desireé's neck. Her whole body was on fire with anger. She had never wanted to beat down one of her crew members until now. She took a step back and let out a breath to compose herself. The crew also stepped back and tried to come to terms with what almost went down. They gave each other high fives with excitement. They loved a good fight even if it was going to be in their own crew.

Jazz angrily pointed at Desireé and yelled, "You know you need to apologize! You took things too far!"

Desireé massaged her neck and looked over at Patience and said, "I'm sorry. I didn't mean to disrespect you. I just don't want to see B.G.R. break up."

Patience put her face within inches of Desireé's and with a stern tone of voice said, "It's already done. Live with it."

Desireé had apologized to Patience but her heart wasn't in it. She had to force herself to calm down because she felt like exploding from the inside out.

Patience, on the other hand, did explode and nearly broke Desireé's neck in the process. Before leaving the crew for the night Patience said, "We need to roll out before the park rangers come by and do a sweep and some of you end up downtown. I'll see you guys tomorrow."

Not waiting for a response from the crew, the two sisters made their way to the parking lot, climbed inside Patience's car and headed home for the night.

Chapter Two

Denim arrived at her best friend, Patrice Fontenot's house like clockwork on the afternoons she didn't have to work so she could see Patrice's infant son, Alejandro. Patrice and Denim had been friends since preschool, but not without trials and tribulations. Over the past year, the two friends had been estranged, which started when Patrice announced her pregnancy. Denim was hurt and disappointed that her friend was so careless. Their pact of attending college together was now nothing but a distant memory and Denim cut all ties with her former friend. That was until an infection set up in Patrice's body, putting her into a coma that nearly cost her her life and the life of her son.

Weeks passed before Patrice came out of the coma. When she did, she had some memory loss, which included the rift between her and Denim. Thankfully, she had made a full recovery and her son was as healthy as he could be and Denim nor her family and friends told her about the feud.

When Denim walked in the house it was as neat as usual except for two baskets of clean laundry sitting on the floor in front of the sofa. Patrice had been folding laundry until Denim arrived. Having her friend there gave her an excuse to take a break and to catch up on things at school. Alejandro was lying in his bassinet, wide-awake and looking up at his mother and her best friend as they greeted each other. Patrice had been homeschooled since she became pregnant but she couldn't wait to go back to Langley High.

"Girl! I love that outfit!"

"Thank you. I bought it the other day," she revealed as she modeled the two-piece yellow Capri pantsuit with matching sandals. "When I saw it I knew I had to have it."

"Well, when I drop these last fifteen pounds you're going to have to let me borrow it."

"You can probably wear it now," Denim stated as she picked Alejandro up and gave him a kiss on the cheek. She cradled him lovingly in her arms before sitting down on sofa next to Patrice.

Patrice pulled the tag out of the collar and asked, "What size is it?"

"It's a size six."

Patrice threw her hands up in the air and said, "Oh, no! I'm not a six yet, but I'm a ten. Give me a few more weeks and I'll be able to squeeze my big butt into it."

The two friends giggled at her comment.

"Stop stressing over your weight. You look good to me, considering what you went through. What did you gain, about twenty-five pounds?" Denim asked and she softly caressed the baby's cheek.

"Girl, please!" Patrice replied as she stood and made her way into the kitchen. She opened the refrigerator and pulled out two bottles of Pepsi and then grabbed Alejandro's bottle out of the bottle warmer. She handed the Pepsi to Denim and sat the baby bottle on the coffee table. She took a sip of her Pepsi and turned to Denim.

"When I was in that coma my body held a lot of fluid. I blew up almost fifty pounds."

"You didn't look like it."

"Well, I was. I've lost thirty pounds but I still have a long way to go."

The two friends spent the next hour or so talking and just spending quality time together. They watched as Alejandro dozed off to sleep and then woke up again with a slight cry for a diaper change and milk. DeMario was the father of Patrice's baby. Even though he was a teen father, he was a good one. Patrice's father had helped him gain employment at the automotive plant, where he worked after school. He was a hands-on dad and loved both Patrice and his son very much. Having a son so early in their lives had delayed many of their plans but it hadn't changed them. College was still definitely on their itinerary so both of them could obtain careers instead of just jobs.

The lifelong friends laughed together as they watched an episode of the reality show *Baldwin Hills* together. Alejandro smiled up at Denim as she placed another bottle of milk into his mouth. Patrice watched quietly as Denim talked to and held her son lovingly. Minutes later, Denim sat the baby bottle on the coffee table and put Alejandro on her shoulder and gently patted his back. When he let out a loud burp she kissed his cheeks again and said, "That was a good burp, Alejandro. You are such a handsome young man."

He smiled as if he understood what she said.

"Patrice, he's growing so fast. I could hold him in my arms all day long."

"Between you, Daddy, DeMario's momma and my momma, I don't know who's spoiling him the most," she replied as she picked up some baby blankets and started folding them.

Denim smiled and said, "It's our job to spoil him. He's so cute and cuddly."

"Yes he is, just like his daddy."

"I didn't say all that," Denim replied jokingly as she rocked him in her arms.

Silence fell over the two momentarily as they continued to watch the reality show. It didn't take long for Alejandro to fall asleep in Denim's arms once again. She eased him into his bed and then grabbed a handful of baby clothes and began to help her friend with the laundry.

"DeMario told me he ran into you the other night and you were somewhere you had no business," Patrice announced.

"DeMario talks too much," Denim replied without making eye contact with her.

Patrice threw a baby bib at Denim and angrily asked, "What the hell were you doing messing around in Scotland Heights? Do you have a death wish or something?"

"Of course not, but I had to find Patience."

Denim went on to explain to Patrice the urgency of finding Patience. As she laid everything out to her, Denim could see that Patrice wasn't registering her need to put her life in danger. Once she finished, Patrice pointed her freshly manicured finger at her.

"You'd better stay away from that girl before you get caught up in some mess. You know B.G.R. has a bad reputation."

"They're not all bad. Patience is actually cool," Denim suggested with somewhat of a smile in her tone of voice. "Did you know she was an honor student?"

"Yes, I heard, but that still don't make up for her being involved with B.G.R along with the rest of those other delinquents."

"I can take care of myself."

Patrice picked up a stack of baby blankets and walked into her bedroom without responding to Denim. When she returned, she had another basket of fresh laundry to fold. She sat the basket on the floor in front of the sofa and took her seat once again next to Denim. Patrice loved her best friend but right now she was very upset with her. Denim didn't always think things through when she was trying to save the world and this thing was a perfect example.

"Whatever you had to tell Patience, you could've waited and told her at school."

"No, it couldn't wait," Denim replied as she stood and picked up their empty Pepsi bottles and threw them into a nearby trash can.

"Why not?" Patrice asked.

"Because I wouldn't be able to live with myself if something happened to her before I had a chance to warn her."

"That's cool, but what would you have done if somebody had put a gun in your face for that shiny little Mustang of yours?"

"Nothing happened, Patrice."

"Maybe not this time, but it was still a stupid move. You bet not let your parents find out you was up there."

Denim had to agree with Patrice on that one. If her parents knew she had been in Scotland Heights she would be on house arrest for a long, long time. It was the closest neighborhood to Langley with a violent past and present and there was little indication things would change for the better anytime soon.

"Not all the people who live there are bad people, Patrice."

"I'm not judging them, but you have to admit that it's a rough area and if anybody knows, De-Mario does. He used to live there with his grand-mother, remember?"

Denim snapped her fingers and said, "That's exactly my point."

"I agree, but the majority of people up there are low-income, fast-moneymaking hoodlums."

Patrice reached over and took Denim's hand and softly said, "I don't want anything to happen to you."

"I know and I feel the same way about you."

The two friends released each other and stood. That's when they noticed a very unpleasant odor coming from the bassinet. They couldn't tell if it was gas or if Alejandro had actually soiled his dia-per.

Patrice giggled and said, "Momma's work is never done."

Denim also giggled and held her nose to keep from breathing the tart fumes coming from Alejan-dro's diaper.

Patrice pointed into the kitchen and said, "There's

a magnet on the refrigerator from Papa John's pizza. Momma left me twenty-dollars so I could order a pizza. I hope you can hang around and help me eat it."

"I can't today. I have tons of homework to do," Denim revealed. "Do you still like pepperoni with extra cheese?"

"Don't change the subject. You're not fooling me, Denim Mitchell. I know you're trying to get out of here so you can go see Dré."

Denim followed Patrice into the bedroom and said, "I wish. You know he's at basketball practice."

"He won't be at practice all night, though," Patrice reminded her as she changed Alejandro's diaper.

Dré was an outstanding and all-American basketball player and had actually made national headlines regarding not only his accomplishments on the basketball court, but off the court as well. He was a gifted painter and had used his talent on both a personal and business level. He'd painted murals in schools and at businesses around town, allowing him to make a lucrative income in the process.

Patrice was a little disappointed that Denim couldn't stay longer but she realized that she didn't

get to be an honor-roll student by chance and success in the classroom would someday reward her
with a full academic scholarship to the college of
her choice.

"Are you sure you can't stay?" Patrice asked as
she put powder on Alejandro's soft bottom and put
a clean diaper on him.

"I'm sure."

Just then, Denim received a text message. She
looked at the cell phone screen and smiled.

"Let me guess . . . that was Dré, huh?" Patrice
asked.

Blushing, Denim said, "He was just letting me
know he was on his way home from practice."

Patrice picked up Alejandro and placed him on
her shoulders and smiled.

"Dré has it bad for you, girl."

"Whatever! Let me call in your pizza order for
you. I'll stay until it's delivered since your hands
are full with that handsome man of yours."

Patrice followed Denim back into the family
room where they folded the rest of the laundry
while they waited for the pizza to arrive. Within
forty minutes, the pizza was delivered and Denim
was able to finally head home so she could start on
her homework.

Chapter Three

Patience had been lying across the bed, staring at her advanced physics textbook for over thirty minutes. Her room was neat as usual and she had her familiar vanilla-scented candles burning, making it easier for her to concentrate. In the next room Jazz was singing loudly and dancing wildly to the hip-hop music booming from her stereo. Patience rolled over and hit on the wall with her fist to get her sister's attention.

"Jazz! Turn down the music! I'm trying to do my homework!"

Patience heard the volume lower and then Jazz burst into her room.

"I'm sorry, sis, I didn't know you were studying. Is that better?"

"Much better," Patience replied as she stood up and walked across the room to get her notebook. Dressed in only a New York Giants T-shirt and royal blue bikini panties, her long, shapely legs looked like they went on for miles.

"Hey sis, do you mind putting on some clothes? Red Rum is going to drop by in a few."

She laid back across her bed and picked up her lead pencil and calculator.

"Why do I have to get dressed? I'm in my room minding my own business. You know Momma don't want him in her house."

"He's not spending the night," Jazz answered as she walked over to the mirror and smoothed down her hair.

"You really could do so much better. Red Rum is the kind of guy that will make it hard for you to get rid of. All he's going to do is use you up and throw you away like yesterday's trash."

Jazz laughed.

"Don't hate. You know Red Rum would never throw me away."

Patience looked at her sister in disbelief. She was

well aware that it was more common than uncommon for roughnecks like Red Rum to change girlfriends as often as they changed their clothes, but for some odd reason, he had kept Jazz around for nearly a year. There was always the possibility that he had other girls on the side, but Red Rum was also well aware that Jazz was not a typical girl and there would be hell to pay if she found out otherwise.

"I'm not hating, Jazz, I'm just keeping it real."

"He loves me."

Now it was Patience's turn to laugh.

"Uh, yeah. He loves what he can get from you and nothing more. Guys like Red Rum aren't capable of love. You need someone you can have a future with, someone who cares about you and your dreams."

Jazz sat on the foot of Patience's bed and looked around her sister's room. They'd had this conversation many times before and it always ended the same. She was left with her feelings slightly hurt while Patience chipped away at her happiness. Red Rum did make her happy and that's all that mattered to her.

"What makes you such an authority? Oh, yeah, I forgot. You have firsthand experience with Don Juan Shawn."

Shawn was a former boyfriend of Patience who was caught with a large amount of drugs in the trunk of his car. She had planned to testify on his behalf until his drug-dealing friend, known on the streets as Pit Bull, threatened to harm her and her family if she did. While she wasn't one to be intimated, she wasn't about to let anyone harm her family and would protect them by any means necessary. Therefore, Shawn sat in jail where he waited for his appeal, leaving Patience heartbroken and guilty. Sadly, before he could appeal his conviction, he was stabbed to death in a jail-yard fight, cutting his young life short. It took her a while to get over the pain and there were times she thought she would never be able to love again.

Patience looked up at Jazz with a glare that warned her not to go any further on the subject.

"Don't start, Jazz."

"Why not? You're always ragging on my man. Why can't we talk about Shawn?"

Patience punched the buttons extra hard on her calculator as she tried to ignore her annoying sister.

"There's a lot you don't know, so drop it," she urged Jazz, but being the pest she could be, sometimes she pushed the issue.

"I don't want to drop it. I want to know what you're hiding."

"Damn! Jazz! Shut up!" Patience yelled.

"I don't want to shut up," Jazz answered as she reached over quickly and snatched Patience's textbook. It was obvious that Patience was keeping secrets from her and she wanted to know what it was.

"Give me the book," Patience asked as she held out her hand.

Jazz smiled and then said, "Not until we finish talking."

Patience slammed her fist down on the bed and quickly stood.

"I'm not going to ask you again."

Jazz was severely taunting Patience and she knew that she had a short temper, especially when it came to her homework or her personal life. Bringing Shawn up wasn't a subject she wanted to talk about.

Jazz held the book out to her sister and said, "Here, take your book."

Patience snatched the textbook out of Jazz's hand and cursed her out.

Jazz laughed and yelled, "You need a maintenance man!"

Patience sat down on her bed and thumbed through her physics book until she found her homework assignment.

"You know, it wouldn't hurt you to pick up a book every now and then instead crawling around under Red Rum."

Jazz walked slowly out the door and before pulling the door closed said, "Don't hate the player, hate the game, sis."

Patience jumped off the bed and locked her bedroom door behind Jazz. She laid across the bed and tried to get her mind off Shawn and Jazz and back on physics. Unfortunately, it wasn't working. So much was going through her mind, especially some of the things Jazz had said to her. She closed her book and pulled a small picture out of the nightstand of her and Shawn. As she laid there staring at it, she reminisced on how close they were and how his arrest seemed like only yesterday.

While hanging out at the lake with a group of friends, they were approached by his friend, Pit Bull, who asked to borrow his car. Shawn didn't hesitate to give him the keys because he'd loaned him the car on more than one occasion. After the car was returned, Shawn was pulled over by police in Scotland Heights with Patience sitting on the passenger side. Upon search of the vehicle they found a plastic bag full of various drugs in the trunk. Instead of snitching on Pit Bull or admitting to owning the drugs, Shawn was charged and convicted with felony possession with intent to sell narcotics. She wanted to somehow clear Shawn's name but he told her to keep quiet. He knew what Pit Bull was capable of and didn't want Patience to get hurt. Now Shawn was lying cold in a grave because of a series of stupid decisions. He knew what Pit Bull's line of work was but he still entrusted him with his car. His hope was to get out on an appeal but he never got the chance. Even now, she occasionally ran into Pit Bull around the Yard and every time he saw her he laughed or made some type of threatening gesture to her, cementing her silence.

"Stupid!" Patience yelled before tossing the picture back into her nightstand. She walked over to the window and looked out into the night. It was nearly eight o'clock and she knew her mother would be home soon. Most nights she was home by seven but some nights it was later. Her explanation was because she had to work overtime. Now that Patience had seen her with the mystery man she wasn't so sure. Her mother did work a full-time job, but she was also very active at church. She was a member of the choir and the hospitality and singles ministries. That's when it hit Patience that her mom may have met the mystery man at church in the singles ministry.

Headlights from a car snapped Patience out of her thoughts. The lights blinded her temporarily and she knew immediately who it was when she heard the loud music bumping from the stereo. She watched as Red Rum climbed out of the car and noticed that he wasn't alone. Patience walked over to the door and yanked it open.

"Jazz, I want Red Rum and his boy out of here in fifteen minutes!"

As she slammed her door closed she heard Jazz yell, "Okay!"

Patience lay across her bed once again to try to get her mind back in the books. As she studied, she could hear Jazz and her guests laughing in the family room. To help block out their voices she stuck her iPod earphones into her ears and hummed to the smooth sounds of Ledisi. As she mellowed out she was able to get herself back in the groove with her physics but it wasn't long before her studying was interrupted again and all hell broke loose.

Patience felt someone touching the back of her leg, startling her. She rolled over and found a strange guy standing in her bedroom. He had a stupid grin on his face and was dressed in a gray hoodie and baggy jeans. She quickly pulled the earphone out of her ears and jumped off the bed.

"What the hell are you doing in my room?"

The guy put his hands up in defense.

"Chill, baby, I was just coming in to holler at you. I heard you humming and I had to find out who that fly voice belonged to."

Patience reached under her bed and pull out a handgun. She pointed it at him and said, "Looks like breaking and entering to me. I should blow you away."

"Hold up a minute, slim. Don't bite off more than you can chew," he said with a mouthful of gold. "You're not the only one who's strapped," he said as he pulled up his shirt to show her his gun.

Patience quickly yelled for her sister. "Jazz!"

The guy looked at Patience's scantily-clad body and smiled.

"Damn! You're tough and hot! I like that in my shorties. You know how to handle yourself."

Jazz and Red Rum ran into the bedroom and saw that Patience had a look on her face that told them she was about to commit a homicide.

Red Rum stepped forward and said, "Bro, what are you doing? You said you were going to the bathroom. What are you doing in here?"

He grinned and said, "I was just checking things out. I heard her singing so I thought I would pop in to take a peek."

"Patience, put that gun down before you hurt somebody," Jazz pleaded.

"No! I want everybody out of my house, now!"

Jazz turned to Red Rum and said, "I'm sorry, baby, but you're going to have to get your boy and roll out. Patience's not kidding and Momma will be home soon anyway."

Red Rum grabbed his friend by the arm and pulled him toward the hallway.

"Come on, bro. You don't want any part of her, especially when she's pissed off."

"Cool, but I like a little fire in my women. I'm sorry she won't give me a chance because I would love to get tangled up in those long, sexy legs."

"Get out!" Patience yelled and she chambered a

round in her gun to let them know she meant business.

Red Rum smiled and pulled his friend back by the arm. "Man, let's get out of here."

"Come on, baby, I'll walk you to the door," Jazz said to Red Rum.

Jazz turned to Patience and frowned.

Just then, Tyric James, a family friend, stepped into the bedroom, startling everyone.

"What the hell is going on in here?" Tyric asked. "Is everything okay in here?" he asked curiously.

"They were just leaving," Jazz responded.

Twenty-five-year old Tyric James was a member of the local police department's vice unit and a longtime family friend. He was also the best friend of their deceased brother Ryan. After Ryan's death, Tyric became somewhat of a guardian angel to the family. In his line of work it was his job to be familiar with the people on his beat, especially Red Rum and his crew. Since Scotland Heights was a high crime area he dropped by often to check in on the girls to make sure they were okay. Tyric was extremely handsome with his cocoa complexion, huge dimples, neatly trimmed goatee, and long eyelashes. He had the body of well-toned athlete and moved with a sexy swagger and a strong air of confidence.

Angry over the scene he'd walked up on, Tyric yelled, "Put the gun down, Brianna, and put on some clothes!"

Red Rum smiled and said, "Chill, Tyric, we were just leaving."

Tyric got in Red Rum's face and yelled, "Don't tell me to chill! You know you're not supposed to be here."

Tyric knew that Jazz was hanging out with Red Rum and he had tried everything in his power to get her to distance herself from him.

"Damn, Tyric! You don't have to be so hostile," Jazz smarted off to him.

As quick as lightning he grabbed her cheeks and squeezed them.

"That hurts, Tyric. Turn me loose," Jazz pleaded.

Red Rum tugged on his baggy jeans and frowned. "Come on, Tyric. You don't have to grab on my girl like that," he pleaded.

Tyric glared at him and said, "This has nothing to do with you."

Red Rum knew not to test Tyric because he grew up in the Yard as well and wasn't one to cross.

"What's going on, partner?" Tyric's partner also stepped in the room, holding a soda can in his hand. He was a large, dark-skinned man with a shiny bald head who looked more like a middle linebacker for an NFL team. Standing nearly six feet five and weighing about 260 pounds, he was fast on his feet and had a history of chasing down criminals half his age and size. He was a tough and dedicated officer on the outside but he also possessed a sensitive nature when he needed to. His name was Vernon Chipman, but everyone called him V-Chip. He also grew up in Scotland Heights and was just as fearless as Tyric. V-Chip looked at the two young men standing in Patience's bedroom and frowned.

"What are y'all's skinny asses doing up in here?"

V-Chip grabbed Red Rum and his friend by their hoods and pulled them out toward the hallway.

"Come on out of here so I can pat you down! You know you have no business in this house, let alone Brianna's bedroom."

V-Chip pulled the gun off Red Rum's friend and said, "What are you doing with this?"

Tyric looked over at Patience and said, "I thought I told you to put that gun down and get on some clothes."

Patience finally lowered the gun but she still

held it in her hand. Tyric released Jazz and stormed over to Patience and took the gun out of her hand.

He turned to Jazz and said, "Jasmine, I need to talk to your sister. Wait for me in the living room." Jazz rolled her eyes and rubbed her sore cheeks as she walked past Tyric and followed V-Chip and her house guests out into the hallway. He closed Patience's bedroom door and watched as she slid into a pair of shorts.

"Is this Ryan's gun?"

Patience sat down on the bed without responding.

Tyric sat next to her and said, "I asked you a question."

"Yes, it's Ryan's gun," she reluctantly responded. "You knew it before you asked me."

He pulled the clip out of it and slid it in his pocket.

"I thought Selena had all of Ryan's stuff locked up?"

"She did, but I know Ryan would want me to have it."

Tyric shook his head and laughed.

"No, he wouldn't. You're going to get yourself

killed or kill somebody and that would break my heart."

Patience laid her head on Tyric's shoulder and closed her eyes. He reached over and put his hand on her thigh and caressed it.

"Tyric, I've been thinking a lot about Ryan lately. Do you think they'll ever find out who killed him?"

"I'm sure they will. Cold case detectives are still working on it," he revealed. "Somebody will eventually call in a tip or come forward because people up here knew Ryan was cool even though he was a cop."

Patience's heart thumped hard in her chest. Ryan was a sensitive subject and every time she talked about him tears welled up in her eyes. Tyric saw the tears and wondered if something more had happened in her room than he witnessed.

"Did that guy put his hands on you?"

"He's still breathing, isn't he?" she joked.

He chuckled.

"I guess that answers my question. Seriously, Brianna, I'm taking Ryan's gun away from you and giving it back to Selena. Cool?"

"Not cool," she answered. "That leaves me with nothing to protect myself out on the streets."

"That's my job," he answered.

"You can't be with me twenty-four-seven, Tyric. Some of these girls out here really hate me."

"They're just jealous of you because you're so fine," he said before giving her a slow, sizzling kiss.

"What was that for?" she asked. "Not that I'm complaining."

"It wasn't for you. It was for me," he revealed. "I haven't seen you since yesterday. Why don't you get your things and go home with me?" he asked.

"You know I can't. Momma will be home soon and I don't want her wondering where I am."

"She won't have to wonder if you go ahead and tell her about us," he suggested. "I hate sneaking around behind Selena's back with you."

"It's not a good time, baby," she replied as she traced his lips with her finger.

Tyric kissed her on the forehead and stood. He tucked Ryan's gun in his waistband and asked, "Will there ever be a good time, Brianna?"

Patience could tell that Tyric's patience was running thin with their secret love affair.

"Yes, just not now. I'll tell her about us soon."

He stared at her with those mesmerizing eyes, making it hard for him to keep his hands off her when he came around.

"Are you coming home with me or not?" he asked.

"Maybe after Momma goes to bed."

Tyric looked at his watch and said, "It's almost nine o'clock now."

"Then come back and pick me up," she suggested as she snuggled up to him.

"No, come with me now and I'll bring you back home in the morning unless you want me to go ahead and tell your mom what's up between us."

Patience thought about Tyric's offer. She walked over to her dresser and pulled out a pair of sweatpants and pulled them over her shorts.

"Okay, I'll come."

He smiled with satisfaction as she pulled a duffel bag from under her bed and filled it with clothes and other necessities before turning to him.

"Are you serious about not giving me Ryan's gun?"

"We'll talk about it later," he replied as he walked toward the door. "I'm going to talk to Jasmine about that thug before I leave."

"Okay, baby," she replied as she finished packing.

Tyric had another heart-to-heart talk with Jazz about Red Rum and her behavior in general. He was hard on her but in the end he hugged and kissed her and let her know that he was there for her and not to disappoint him. Tyric had a way with words and Jazz knew she was wrong by having the young men in the house. She apologized and told him she would try to do better and make better choices.

Ten minutes after Tyric and V-Chip left, Selena Baxter walked through the door. She was a beautiful woman who looked much younger than her forty-three years. Not many mothers were able to maintain their Coke-bottle figure after having children but Selena had been successful and was often mistaken for her daughters' sister instead of their mother. She resembled the actress Angela Bassett, with her high cheekbones and strong nature.

"Hey, Momma." Jazz greeted her with a kiss and took her purse and grocery bags out of her hands. "You must've worked over tonight."

She sat down in the recliner and smiled.

"Yes, and I'm beat tired. Where's your sister?"

"In her room," she announced. "She's been studying for an exam."

"What about you? Don't you have some homework or something to do?"

"No, ma'm," Jazz lied. "I did it at school."

"What have you been doing all evening?" her mother asked.

"Well . . . I've been . . . you know . . . just messing around, listening to music."

"Uh-huh," Selena replied while studying her youngest daughter's behavior.

"According to Tyric, you've been doing more than listening to music."

Jazz rolled her eyes. Tyric didn't waste any time calling her mother to snitch on her.

"Momma, my friends were only here for about fifteen minutes."

She sat up in the recliner and said, "I don't care if they were here for ten seconds. When I say no boys in this house when I'm not here, that's what I mean. Now, are we going to have to have this conversation again?"

Jazz could see the fire in her mother's eyes.

"No, Ma'm," Jazz replied. "I'm sorry."

Just then, Patience stepped out into the hallway with her duffel bag and book bag on her shoulders. Confused, her mother looked at her and asked, "Where are you going so late?"

"I'm staying over at a friend's house tonight."

"What friend?" Selena asked.

Patience walked toward the door and said, "Just a friend, Momma. It's no big deal."

"Is it a female friend?" she asked.

Jazz folded her arms and waited with anticipation to hear Patience's answer.

Patience turned to her mother.

"No, ma'm, it's a male friend."

"Excuse me, young lady?" Selena replied.

"It's no big deal, Momma; I'm just going to study for my advanced physics exam. We're going to be up late so I'm taking clothes so I can go on to school from there."

Selena laughed.

"Child! Do you think I'm stupid?" she asked. "What makes you think that I'm going to let you spend the night with a *male* friend?"

Patience knew she was taking a chance telling her mother the truth, but she was almost eighteen years old and she wouldn't be able to control her much longer.

"Momma, it's cool. I'm almost eighteen, remember?"

"I knew it!" Jazz yelled. "Patience has a piece on the side."

Patience glared at her sister and said, "You're so ignorant, Jazz!"

Selena pointed at Jasmine and said, "Stop adding fuel to the fire, Jasmine."

Selena walked over and cupped Patience's face.

"Sweetheart, you don't have to remind me that you're almost eighteen. I know that I won't be able to have a say in what you do much longer, but you still live in my house so you will abide by my rules. Understand?"

"But, Momma—"

"No, *buts*, Brianna. You're my daughter and if you come up missing I need to know who you were last seen with. I want to know his name, address, Social Security number, blood type, and everything else about him."

Patience's mind was racing and she knew she had to think fast. She was smart and if she worked things the right way, she could probably get out of the house clean and clear.

"His name is Rick and he lives in Meadow Hills."

"Is that anywhere near Tyric's house?" Selena asked curiously.

"Yes, ma'am."

"You're not spending the night at a stranger's house, but if he lives near Tyric I would feel much better if you stayed with Tyric."

Bingo! Mission accomplished. Her mother had

worked right into the palm of her hand. Now she would end up where she had planned to go all along. Now she was getting to go with her mother's approval.

"I want to call Tyric to see if knows the young man."

Patience opened the front door and said, "okay, may I go now?"

"Yes, Brianna, you may go but call me as soon as you get to Tyric's house."

Patience kissed her mother's cheek and said, "Thank you, Momma. I love you and I'll call you. Good night."

Selena nodded and said, "I love you too, Brianna. Drive carefully."

"I love you too, Momma."

Chapter Four

Tyric swung open the door to his small, ranch-style two-bedroom house.

"You're late."

Patience walked past him and said, "I got here as fast as I could. You're lucky I made it here at all."

Tyric chuckled as he closed the door behind her. He put his arm around her waist and then revealed to Patience the conversation he had with her mother regarding the imaginary friend, Rick. As they walked into the family room Patience could tell by his tone of voice that he felt guilty lying to her mother. He was tired of the lies but because he was in love with her, he continued to keep quiet until she felt it was a good time to tell Selena about their relationship.

He took the over night bag out of her hands and said, "I'm glad you're here."

"Me too," she replied as she sat down on the sofa and pulled one of her textbooks out of the book bag.

Tyric disappeared into his bedroom with her bag and returned with a newspaper under his arm.

"Momma really trusts you, Tyric. I really can't believe she let me stay over."

He sat down beside her and said, "Well, that will probably end once she finds out we've been lying to her all this time."

Patience closed her eyes and said, "Not tonight, Tyric, please."

He put his hands up in surrender. This was a sensitive subject between the couple but he didn't want to ruin the night arguing about it.

Patience opened her textbook in silence and started reading.

"Big test tomorrow?" he asked as he scanned over the sports section of the newspaper.

She nodded without making eye contact with him.

He sat the newspaper on the sofa and said, "I'm sorry. I didn't mean to upset you as soon as you got here."

"It's okay. You're right about telling Momma anyway."

Tyric reached over and caressed her cheek to comfort her. He wanted his home to be a place of relaxation for her so he did best to remove the tension between them.

"How long have you been studying for your test?"

She rubbed her tired, red eyes and said, "About three hours."

He took the book out of her hands and sat it on the coffee table.

"It's been a long day, you're exhausted and you have school tomorrow. I'm sure you've studied enough. Come on so you can get some sleep."

He stood and pulled her up into his arms. "Let's call Selena and let her know you made it safely and then you're mine for the rest of the night."

Patience wrapped her arms around his neck and nuzzled her face against his warm neck. He did know how to make her feel secure and the fresh scent of his aftershave sped up the rhythm of her heart. She yawned.

"Tyric?"

"Yes, dear," he answered jokingly.

"I think I'm ready to go to bed now," she whispered seductively.

"It would be my pleasure."

Patience was so tired that after she got out of the shower she fell asleep within minutes of laying her head on the pillow. The room was illuminated by the bright moonlight shining through the windows and Tyric couldn't help but be mesmerized by her beauty. As he lay there listening to the sound of her breathing, he envisioned this scene on a more permanent level, which made his heart overflow with love. Tonight, he would let her rest, but the moment the sun peeked through the windows, he would partake in a sensual exploration of his sweetheart's soft, six-foot frame.

The next morning Patience and Tyric had to rush to get dressed after a quick breakfast of waffles and sausage links. They had laid in each other's arms as long as possible before finally crawling out of bed so they could start their day. As Tyric listened to the morning traffic report while he laced up his Timberland boots, Patience plugged in her flat iron before gazing out the bedroom window. In the morning sunlight she noticed the dew that had accumulated on the windshield of her car and that the trees were beginning to turn colors, signifying the beginning of fall, her favorite time of the year.

"I think Momma has a boyfriend."

He laughed.

"Are you serious?"

"I saw her in the park the other night in the car with a man. They were kissing and everything."

He buttoned up his sky blue shirt and picked up his wallet.

"Selena's a fine woman and she's still young. It wouldn't surprise me," he said as he checked to make sure he had all the contents. "What did he look like?"

"I don't know. I guess he looked normal," she explained. "I'm thinking she may have met him at church."

"Well, she's probably been dating him for a while if they were locking lips."

Patience ran the flat iron through a section of her hair, giving it a nice, shiny sheen.

"I wonder why she hasn't mentioned him?"

"Probably the same reason you haven't told her about us," he replied as he picked up his badge, which hung on a chain. He tucked it discreetly underneath his shirt.

Patience imagined the loneliness her mother was probably experiencing and it made her heart ache for her.

"She hasn't dated anybody since Daddy died."

"I'm sure Selena misses the company of a man just like any widow would. You don't have a problem with it, do you?"

"No, as long as he's cool, loves my momma, and don't mistreat her."

"I'm happy for Selena. She deserves another good man."

"Can you check him out, Tyric? I have his license plate number," she revealed as she pulled the small piece of paper out of her book bag.

Tyric took the paper out of her hand and said, "Yeah, I'll run a check on him."

She caressed his face before walking over to the mirror to check her appearance.

"Thank you, baby. I just need to know this dude is cool."

When she looked up, she noticed Tyric smiling at her.

"What are you smiling at?"

"I'm looking at you in those jeans," he answered

as he tucked the slip of paper into his pocket. "They were made for you."

The jeans she wore were a pair of Dereon jeans, which she found to fit her long legs and curvy hips with precision. She walked over to Tyric and gave him a thank-you kiss before she finished packing the rest of her belongings. He complimented her often and she made sure they never went unrewarded with a kiss.

"Speaking of the park," he asked. "Were you there with those girls?"

Patience continued to run the flat iron through her hair until she had it exactly like she wanted it. She ignored his question for a few seconds, but she knew she wouldn't be able to avoid it altogether. Tyric had changed gears on their whole conversation and now she was sure they were going to be late.

She opened a tube of lipstick, smoothed it over her lips and calmly said, "Baby, you know the deal."

He walked over to her, took her by the arm and gently turned her around to face him.

"And you know I'm a cop," he reminded her. "I love you, Brianna, but no matter what, I have to do my job."

She put her hands on her hips and asked, "What

are you saying? Are you going to arrest me or something?"

He folded his arms and asked, "Do I have a reason to?"

She turned back to the mirror and said, "You know what it's like growing up in the Yard."

Tyric sat down in a nearby chair and put his small-caliber handgun into his ankle strap. "Of course I know. That's why I became a cop in the first place so I could try and make a difference."

"Things are different now, Tyric, you don't—"

He pointed his finger at her angrily as he stood. "Don't talk to me like I don't know what's up! I grew up in those streets and I work them everyday and I swear to God if I ever catch you, Jazz, or any of those others knuckleheads doing anything illegal I will take you in."

By growing up in Scotland Heights, Tyric understood how difficult it was to stay out of trouble. It was a survival trap most teens fell into and was quite common in Anytown, USA. Tyric had first-hand knowledge about the gang life because when he was a teen he was also pressured to join. However, playing sports and having a strict father made it easier for him to steer clear. The situation was a little different for girls, especially when there was no father around. No matter how tough a mother was—and Selena was tough—there was only so much she could do to control her daughters.

Patience stared at Tyric in disbelief. Tyric's words were heated and his expression was serious. She never believed he would ever turn her in but her association with B.G.R. was the one thing that got his blood boiling. She knew he loved her and she could see the pain in his face every time she mentioned anything about B.G.R. But leaving a gang wasn't something a crew member just did and he knew that.

Her brother Ryan had tried his best to keep the sisters out of gangs and now that he was deceased, Tyric picked up where he left off. That's why he made it his duty to look after them after their brother was murdered. Now finally a senior in high school, Patience could see the light at the end of the tunnel. She was well on her way to graduating with honors and obtaining a full college scholarship. It would be her ticket out of the hood and out of B.G.R. for good. She just prayed she would be able to leave unscathed because Tyric was the love of her life and she didn't want to lose him.

She cupped his handsome face and said, "You know I've been in B.G.R. for five years and now I'm the queen. There's a protocol that I have to follow, baby, but I promise that I won't do anything that will make you have to put your cuffs on me, officially that is."

Patience couldn't help but throw in a little reminder of the games they'd played during intimacy that involved his cuffs. He was trying to have a serious conversation with her but mentioning the cuffs made him have flashbacks of some of their sensual adventures at his house.

He hugged her waist and said, "That was smooth. You think you're slick by slipping in that remark about my cuffs. You're good, Brianna. I see why you're over your crew. I don't like it, but I understand."

She pushed away from him and picked up her cell phone. As she checked her text messages she said, "B.G.R. hasn't been all bad, Tyric. In fact, if it hadn't been for my crew, there were a couple of times that I could've been—"

He put his hand up to stop her. He really didn't want to know any particular details. Tyric worked in vice but he was very knowledgeable of the various gangs and their illegal activities. Fortunately for Patience, B.G.R. had been an insignificant gang to the gang unit because they were one of the least violent gangs in the area.

He looked at his watch and picked up his other handgun and slid it into the holster on his waist. "Listen, we can talk about this later," he announced as he pulled her lovingly into his arms. "We have to get out of here before we're both late. Okay?"

She hugged his waist tightly and softly replied, "Okay."

He titled her chin so he could look into her beautiful brown eyes. "I do love you, Brianna. If I didn't I wouldn't be so hard on you. I'm only trying to protect you."

She kissed his chin and then his lips and said, "I know, baby, and I love you too."

Tyric gave her one last kiss before giving her a soft pat on the backside. "Let's go and make sure you call Selena on the way to school."

Patience picked up her book bag while Tyric grabbed her overnight bag. She followed him out the door and into the driveway where they drove off in separate directions to start yet another exciting day.

Chapter Five

Denim pulled into the student parking lot earlier than normal. As she sat in her car she pulled out her diary and decided to record a few lines.

> *Dear Diary,*
> *It's been awhile since I wrote anything but my life has been on fast-forward. I went up to Scotland Heights and warned Patience about some girls in her crew who are plotting to set her up. Why? I don't know and neither does Patience. On another note I've*

been spoiling Alejandro. He's a sweetheart and I love hanging out with Patrice again. Dré is deep in basketball so we haven't had a chance to hang out as much. Work is good but busy and I'm loving the extra money. I have my eye on a pair of leather boots with the matching purse and in a few more weeks, they'll be all mine.

Later,
D

Denim closed her diary and slid it back into her book bag. She exited her vehicle and made her way across the parking lot toward the school. As she got closer, she was surprised to find Patience sitting all alone on the hood of her car studying.

"Good morning, Patience."

Patience looked up from her book and smiled.

"What's up, Mitchell."

"I'm glad to see you're okay."

Patience closed the textbook and said, "Yeah, I'm cool. So far no one has been stupid enough to step to me."

Denim was happy to see that Patience hadn't let the sinister plot against her affect her academics.

"Are you getting ready for a test or something?"

Nodding, Patience replied, "advanced physics."

"I'm scared of you," Denim said jokingly.

Patience slid off the hood of her car and said, "Don't even try to front. Those honor classes will be a no-brainer for you too."

Giggling, Denim answered, "I guess. They are a challenge, though."

Patience reached inside her car and pulled out her book bag. She put her textbook inside it and swung it over her shoulders.

"The bell is about to ring. We'd better head in."

"I'll be in shortly. I'm waiting for someone," Denim revealed as she scanned the parking lot.

"Who? Your sweetie, Dré?" Patience teased.

Denim blushed.

"Maybe."

Patience laughed and said, "I'm not mad at you. You two make a cute couple."

"Thanks."

"Well, I'll see you around," Patience replied before walking off. "Don't be late."

"I won't. Patience, before you go I just want to say if you still want me to help you find out who those girls are, I will."

"You do know you don't have to help me. I mean, I will eventually find out who they are."

"But you'll find out faster with my help," Denim explained. "I'll keep my ears open around school and if somebody's voice sounds familiar I'll let you know."

"Okay," Patience replied as she backed away. "See you later, Mitchell."

"Good-bye."

Denim watched Patience walk across the parking lot and enter the school. She checked her watch and realized that Dré was running late so she started walking toward the school's entrance. When she got within a few feet of the entrance Dré honked his horn as he pulled into a parking space. Denim smiled and walked back out into the parking lot and waited for him to exit the vehicle, but instead of getting out of the car, he motioned for her to come over to him.

She quickly ran over to his car and said, "Dré, we're going to be late to class if you don't hurry."

He climbed out of the car and gave Denim a hug and kiss on the lips. The scent of his cologne hypnotized her.

"Let's skip."

"Skip? Are you crazy?" she asked as she looked toward the school.

"Come on, Denim. Let's do something wild for a change. We don't have to skip the whole day, just the first couple of hours. We haven't had a chance to spend any time together lately and it's about to kill me."

Denim thought for a moment and said, "If my parents find out, they'll go ballistic."

"What's new? Beside, you're creative and they won't know if you don't tell them. I know you can come up with something to tell them just in case they find out."

She took a step back and asked, "So you want me to start lying to them again?"

With a big grin on his face he said, "No, baby, just for today. They're at work, aren't they?"

Denim heard the first bell ring.

"Yes, they're at work, but you know how they are. It took them a long time to start trusting me again."

"Just tell them you had a flat tire or something," he suggested.

Denim thought for a moment and then said, "They're going to want to know why I didn't call them."

"Just explain to them that you had the flat down

the street from the school. Let them know that you're trying to be independent and don't want to call them for every little problem."

She poked him in the chest with her finger and said, "You'd better be right, Dré."

"I know I'm right. All you have to do is call them when we get back. It'll be a couple of hours before the attendance office reports your absence."

"You know they're going to check to see if you were late too," she pointed out.

"They shouldn't mind knowing I'm the one who helped you get your tire fixed. I have no problem going through the motions with you so we can have proof."

She giggled.

"You're serious about this, aren't you?"

"I'm serious about you, so I'll do anything to be with you. Basketball has taken up a lot of my time lately and I want to make it up to you."

"What exactly do you have in mind?" she asked as she snuggled up to him.

He leaned in close to her ear and whispered, "I'd rather show you than tell you."

Dré's warm breath sent shivers over her body. He was right about one thing. They hadn't been to-gether in a while and maybe today would be just what they needed to get their relationship back on track and smoking hot once again.

Dré looked nervously toward the school and said, "Well, if we're going to do this we'd better leave before the resource officer spots us and make us go inside."

"Are you driving?" she asked.

Dré walked her to her car and opened her door for her.

"Since I plan to sabotage your tire for real to cover our tracks you need to follow me. We have about two and half hours to get everything done and I want to spend most of that time with you."

"So where are we going?" Denim asked as she climbed inside her car.

"Somewhere very, very private," he replied as he winked at her before backing away. "Just follow me."

Minutes later, Dré pulled inside the garage of his home and Denim pulled her car in beside him. He lowered the garage door and quickly climbed out. Denim sat in her car and tried to swallow the lump in her throat, but she was having difficulty.

"Are you okay?" he asked as he opened her car door.

"My throat's a little dry," she replied as she put her hand up to her throat.

"Come inside so you can get something to drink. You're not getting nervous on me, are you?" he asked with a gleam in his eyes.

"No way," she lied.

Denim exited the vehicle and asked, "Are you sure your parents aren't here?"

"I'm sure," he answered as he walked over to his father's workbench and picked up a screw.

"What are you doing?" Denim asked.

"Giving you a flat tire," he answered with a smile.

Denim watched as Dré picked up a hammer and pushed the nail into the tread of her back tire. He then let the air out to speed up the process.

"There! You officially have a flat tire."

Denim looked at the tire and said, "This is crazy."

Dré unlocked the door to the kitchen and deactivated the alarm system.

"It's not crazy, we're being creative."

"If you say so," Denim replied as she followed him into the house. He looked so handsome in his neatly pressed jeans and red button-down shirt. His athletic shoes looked brand new and he took great pride in his appearance.

What Dré hadn't thought about was whether his mother had installed a hidden camera in their new home like she claimed she had in their old home. He never really believed her and only thought she told him to keep him on his toes. Today, he didn't care if it was true. All he wanted was a chance to be with Denim and love her like he used to love her before their lives changed.

"Want a Pepsi?" Dré asked as he opened the refrigerator.

"Yes, thanks. My throat is so dry."

Dré opened the soda for Denim and handed it to her. He couldn't help but stare at her shapely body, especially the way the low-rise jeans were hugging her hips.

"Here you go."

Denim quickly gulped the soda and then threw the bottle into the trash can.

"Dang, girl, were you that thirsty?" he asked.

"Something like that," she replied before letting out a loud burp. Denim put her hand over her mouth and said, "I'm so sorry. That slipped out."

Dré laughed and then pulled her into his arms.

"Apology accepted," he whispered before kissing her softly on the neck.

She breathlessly purred, "Dré."

"We don't have much time," he whispered as he took her hand and led her down the hallway to his room, "Are you ready?"

"As ready as I'm going to be."

When they stepped into his room she noticed he had several pair of jeans and shirts laid out on the chair. It appeared that he'd had some difficulty making up his mind on what outfit to wear this morning. As she looked around she saw his closet door standing wide open. At the bottom of the closet were two shelves lined with various footwear, including boots and athletic shoes.

She picked up one of the shirts and said, "Looks like somebody had a hard time getting dressed this morning."

"Just a little bit," he answered as he took the shirt out of her hand and quickly hung it back up before closing his closet door. He immediately turned his attention back to her as he cupped her face and stroked her cheek with his thumbs.

"You do know you're my girl, right?"

Denim hugged his waist lovingly. "Yeah, I know."

Dré lowered his mouth to hers and kissed her tenderly as he slowly unbuttoned the pink blouse she had on. When he pushed it off her shoulders and revealed the pink-laced bra she had on underneath, he couldn't help but stare at her beautiful brown skin.

"You are so hot."

She blushed.

"I don't think so. I'm just me."

Dré sat down on the bed, pulling Denim into his lap, "That's what I love about you. You don't even know how special you are."

She tugged at his shirt and said, "Dré, I lied when I said I wasn't nervous."

"It's okay. I'm a little nervous myself."

Dré held her hand and then took Denim on a short journey of adolescent passion. The love they carried in their hearts for each other radiated in every kiss shared, every word spoken and the caress of their hands. It was hard for Dré to visualize himself with any other girl or Denim with any other guy. They were too close and from the moment they crossed the line of intimacy that first time over a year ago, they were totally committed to each other.

Denim closed her eyes and planted butterfly kisses on Dré's ample lips and face as she laid in his arms.

"That was off da hook," she whispered. "I thought I was going to die."

"You and me both," he admitted as he pulled her even closer to his body.

"Seriously, Dré, I don't think any other guy can love me like you do. We're connected emotionally and spiritually."

He frowned.

"I don't even want to think about you kicking it with another guy. Change the subject."

She smiled.

"I love it when my baby's jealous," she teased as she massaged his shoulders.

"I'm jealous, but I trust you."

"I trust you too, Dré."

Denim looked around Dré's room at the Michael Jordan poster and some of his trophies on one wall. On another wall were several pieces of his most prized artwork. One painting in particular was new. She pointed at the painting, which looked like a sketch of a young female and male holding a baby. He'd already started adding colorful oil paint to the baby, but had left the other figures untouched.

"Is that a painting of Alejandro?"

"Yeah, but it's not finished yet. I haven't decided if I wanted to make Patrice and DeMario silhouettes or not. What do you think?"

"I love Patrice and DeMario but I think Alejandro should be the star of the painting. I'm sure that whatever you come up with they'll love it."

Looking at the painting reminded Denim how gifted Dré was as an artist. His renditions were so lifelike and he mastered every detail of people when he painted their likeness.

She wrapped her arms around his neck and said, "I could stay like this forever."

"Me too," he agreed before running his hand through her thick auburn hair. "You and everything about you feels so right."

"I feel the same way, Dré," she said as she kissed the center of his muscular chest.

He quickly rolled over and sat up on the side of the bed.

"You'd better stop before we end up missing third-period class too. We have to get out of here so we can get your tire changed."

Denim giggled as she stood and gathered her apparel.

"You know, we could get in a lot of trouble if anybody finds out the real reason wc cut class."

"We're cool, Denim," he assured her. "We just have to make sure we don't make this a habit. I can't have your pops chasing me down the street with a gun."

She laughed when she got a visual of Dré running from her father. It wasn't too far from the truth because Denim's father had talked to Dré man-to-man on many occasions about the dos and don'ts of dating his daughter. In fact, his own father had talked to him about being careful and by most accounts he'd abided by Mr. Mitchell's rules. However, young love was too strong for the young couple to be held back by parental rules.

Dré looked at the time on his cell phone and said, "We have to get out of here so we can get your tire fixed."

Denim agreed before she ran into the bathroom for a quick shower. Dré followed once she was finished and they hurried out the door and to the tire shop before heading back to school.

Chapter Six

Denim sat in her third-period class daydreaming about her morning session with Dré. Patience noticed she wasn't paying attention and threw a wad of paper at her, hitting her arm.

Denim turned and whispered, "What?"

"Stop daydreaming and pay attention," Patience whispered back to her.

"I'm not daydreaming," Denim replied softly.

Seconds later Denim was daydreaming once again. Luckily, the teacher didn't call on her to answer any questions. In the end she gave the class a pop quiz, saving Denim from definite embarrassment.

* * *

When the final bell rang, Denim made her way out of the school along with the hundreds of other students. As she hurried out into the parking lot she was nearly knocked down by a couple of girls who didn't seem to be paying attention or care that they were pushing people out of their way.

"Don't you know how to say *excuse me*!" Denim yelled before she realized who she was talking to.

A girl by the name of Desireé turned to Denim and pointed at herself and asked, "Are you talking to me?"

"No, Desireé, maybe she was talking to me," another girl by the name of Kayla answered as she stepped forward in front of Desireé.

Denim immediately realized she was outnumbered. She also realized these girls were the voices she heard plotting against Patience at the deli. Denim looked over the gathering crowd to see if Patience might happen to be among them, but unfortunately she was nowhere in sight so she did what anyone would expect her to do . . . face them and deal with whatever came next.

Denim stepped up to the girl named Kayla and said, "I think you owe me an apology."

By now the small crowd of students who had noticed the altercation had grown larger. A fight was always good entertainment among students, but a potential catfight was usually the highlight, especially for young teenage boys.

Desireé pointed her finger in Denim's face and said, "You'd better recognize who you're stepping to but if you think you can make us apologize, go right ahead."

"Go right ahead and do what?" Patience asked as she stepped out of the crowd, startling not only Denim but the other two girls as well.

Everyone in the crowd started laughing when they saw the looks on Desireé and Kayla's faces because they knew that Patience could possibly set things off.

"What's going on?" Patience asked as she looked at Kayla and Desireé.

Desireé immediately pointed at Denim and said, "What's going on is that this chick disrespected us by almost knocking us down as we were coming out of school. Then she had the nerve to ask us to apologize to her."

Patience smiled at Denim and then turned to Desireé and Kayla, who were well-known B.G.R. members.

"Is that what happened?" Patience asked Mercedes, a third girl who stood silent among the other two. She nodded in agreement without answering verbally.

Patience knew they were lying but as head of the crew she decided to go along with her crew members, especially since there was a large crowd looking on.

"Well, I'm sure it was an accident. Mitchell's cool, so you guys can squash whatever's going on. No harm, no foul. Right?"

Then before Patience could walk away, Desireé did the unthinkable. She defied Patience startling everyone.

"Wait a minute!" Desireé yelled as she got in Denim's face. "You can't just let her walk! "She ain't going nowhere until she apologizes."

The crowd groaned in anticipation of what would be said or done next.

"I said, let it go!" Patience yelled as she shoved Desireé out of Denim's face.

"Don't put your hands on me, Patience!" Desireé yelled.

"Who do you think you're talking to?" Patience asked as she grabbed Desireé by the arm. "As a matter of fact, get your ass over here and apologize to Mitchell."

"What?" Desireé asked.

Desireé couldn't believe what Patience was doing to her, especially in front of the whole school. It was unprecedented, stunning everyone.

"Don't do it, Desireé," Kayla yelled out in support.

Patience pointed at Kayla and said, "You shut up!"

Denim stood in shock as she watched Patience handled her crew, but Desireé stood relentless, refusing to follow her orders.

"For the last time, Desireé, apologize to Denim!" Patience demanded as she nearly cut the circulation off in her arm.

"Okay! Damn! You're hurting my arm! I'm sorry I bumped into you, Denim!" Desireé said before pulling her arm out of Patience's tight grasp. She pushed her way through the crowd and walked off infuriated. Mercedes quickly followed Desireé but when Kayla turned and walked passed Denim she whispered, "Watch your back."

Patience overheard Kayla's comment and quickly grabbed her by the back of her shirt, stopping her in her tracks.

"What did you say to her?" Patience asked.

"Come on, Patience!" Kayla pleaded. "What

are you doing? She's not B.G.R. Why are you taking her side?"

"Don't worry about it," Patience yelled as she pointed her finger in the center of Kayla's forehead. "Get the hell out of here before you really make me lose my temper!"

Kayla also pushed her way through the crowd and eventually caught up with Desireé and Mercedes farther out in the parking lot. Only then did the large crowd disperse and go on their merry way.

Patience turned to Denim and folded her arms and asked, "What am I going to do with you?"

Denim pulled Patience to the side and anxiously said, "Patience, those were the girls who were talking about you in the deli. That's them! I knew it the minute I heard them talking."

"Are you sure?" Patience asked as she watched them get into Desireé's car and drive away.

"Yes, I'm sure."

"What about Mercedes?" Patience asked. She wanted to know about Mercedes because she was somewhat of a follower. She had more bark than bite, unlike the other two. They could be vicious and determined and a handful if Patience didn't keep them under her watchful eyes.

"I'm not sure about her. She could've been." Denim revealed.

Patience had the information she needed. Now she had to decide what she was going to do with it and how she was going to handle the situation. Now that she had identified who was after her, she needed to know why and what her crew members were plotting. If the need presented itself she might have to strike them before they approached her, especially since she had handled them in front of their classmates. She was sure the incident had only added fuel to whatever fire was burning inside them and it could only get worse from here.

"Thanks for the information, Mitchell, and could you please try and stay out of trouble?"

"Seriously, it wasn't my fault. So what are you going to do now?" Denim asked as they walked toward their cars.

Patience looked over at Denim and said, "That's not for you to worry about, but if you have any more problems out of anybody in my crew, let me know. Okay?"

Surprised by Patience's offer, she nodded and said, "I will. Thanks."

"No, thank you, Mitchell," she replied before

climbing inside her car and pulling out of the parking lot.

Before leaving the parking lot, Denim pulled out her diary and made a second notation for the day. She wanted to record the information while it was still fresh on her mind.

Dear Diary,

I don't know what's going on, but it seems like I'm a magnet for trouble. I nearly got into a brawl with some girls name Desireé, Kayla and Mercedes of B.G.R. Once again, Patience came to my rescue but the good thing that came out of it was that I was able to tell Patience that these were the girls who are plotting against her. I don't know what she's going to do to them but I guess my work is done. On another note, I had a flat tire this morning and Dré took care of it for me. (wink, wink)

D

Several miles away from the school, Desireé, Kayla, and Mercedes pulled into the parking lot of a local pizza joint. Desireé was still fuming from the incident and didn't have much to say to the other two as she drove through town. Once she put the car in park and shut off the engine, she turned to Kayla and asked, "Can you believe what Patience did?"

"No way, she's completely lost her mind. First she orders B.G.R. dissolved and now this? She's crazy," Kayla answered without hesitation.

"What I don't get is why she would defend Denim Mitchell?" Desireé asked as she finally opened her car door and climbed out. "What connection does she have with her?"

"I don't know. It's not like she circulates in our circle," Mercedes replied as they made their way into the local pizza parlor.

Kayla giggled.

"Well, whatever it is, I'm pissed," Desireé admitted. "Patience embarrassed us in front of everybody. How are we going to show our faces at school tomorrow?"

"Don't stress over it, Desireé," Mercedes said to try and comfort her. "By tomorrow something else will go down and everybody will have forgotten all about us."

Mercedes was correct, because in a high school of over two thousand students, there was always some type of drama going on in the hallways, cafeteria, student parking lot or bus platforms. Also, B.G.R wasn't the only gang in the school that laid the foundation for a volatile atmosphere on a daily basis.

The three girls mouths watered as they inhaled the smell of fresh pizza dough and all the fixings. In the corner of the room stood two video poker machines that were being played by a couple of elderly gentleman who had stacks of quarters lined up on the countertop in front of them. They were regulars and could be found in the pizza parlor almost every day, especially since it shared the building with a barbershop.

The girls studied the menu before ordering a large sausage and cheese pizza. They continued to talk about Patience, Denim, the unpredictable future of B.G.R. and the altercation at school. Once the pizza and sodas arrived, the three of them immediately bit into their hot, cheesy slices.

"Are you guys going to ever tell me why you're so mad at Patience?" Mercedes asked.

"We have our reasons, but believe me, they're justified and it's worth every penny," Desireé revealed.

Kayla giggled at Desireé's comment. Mercedes

was new to B.G.R. but she had earned her position in the crew so she wanted them to start trusting her at some point, especially if they were going to continue to let her hang out with them.

"That's all you're going to tell me?" she asked.

"Okay, I'll tell you, but you have to promise not to repeat a word to anybody because if you do, then you'll have me to deal with."

Mercedes nodded in agreement before taking a sip of her soda.

Desireé looked around the room to make sure no one was in earshot of them. Then she laid out the reasoning behind the vendetta against Patience. As Mercedes listened she realized that the facts as they were been told about Patience could happen to anyone, including herself, and it was scary to know that people could be bought for the right price without ever giving the preservation of life and limb a second thought. It was a cold-blooded plan and about the almighty dollar and nothing else.

Mercedes leaned back in her seat and frowned once Desireé had finished laying everything out for her. Desireé took a bite of her pizza as if she'd just finished reciting a poem to the group. There was no animosity and the anger against Patience has disappeared. In fact, she seemed somewhat happy about the whole plot but her eyes lit up the most when they talked about the money that was involved.

Kayla held her hand up so Desireé could give her a high five and yelled, "Baby, we're about to get paid!"

"How much money are you guys getting for doing this?" Mercedes asked.

Desireé picked up another slice of pizza and took a bite. "It's enough to make all our dreams come true and then some."

The information Desireé and Kayla had given Mercedes had shed a bright light onto their motivation against Patience. It wasn't personal, this was strictly business, and it was wrong.

Kayla smiled at Mercedes and asked, "Why do you have that stupid look on your face? You can't sit there and say you wouldn't do the same thing if the opportunity presented itself."

"Look, this is not anything I want to get involved with. It's obvious you guys have everything already worked out and it's not like you want to share any of your money with me anyway, so why do you even need me around?"

Desireé looked at Kayla and then over at Mercedes

and said, "You know what? You're right. Get lost. We don't need you and if you breathe a word of this, your ass will be next on the list. Do you feel me?"

Mercedes stood and said, "Oh, I definitely feel you. Peace!"

Then before walking away she reached across the table and turned over both of their sodas, spilling the cold beverage into their laps.

Chapter Seven

Patience pulled up to the Central City police department and parked her car. As she sat there, she watched as officers mingled outside the building. As she waited for Tyric to emerge, she turned up the volume on her CD player to the sounds of Beyoncé's new CD. She really loved Tyric and the realization that they would be separated once she left for college was beginning to be heavy on her mind. She didn't know how her mother would react to the news of their relationship; he was, after all, seven years older than she was.

Tyric had always had a special place for Patience in his heart but he never wanted to disrespect Ryan by trying to make a move on her until she was older. Patience had made an impression on Tyric long before he ever sought a romantic interest in her. She was beautiful and possessed a strong personality that he looked for in the women he'd previously dated. It wasn't until after Ryan's death that Tyric had the courage to pursue her. He was the first guy she'd dated since Shawn and it scared her. She knew he loved her not only as a friend, but as a woman too, while Shawn loved her in his own way, which was mostly physical. She loved Shawn nevertheless and she was beginning to feel a strong urge to right a wrong that still tainted his memory, but it could cost her dearly. She felt like she was living with a dark cloud over her head and it was weighing heavily on her heart. Shawn's family deserved to know the truth but she wouldn't be able to live with herself if things went bad and her loved ones got hurt.

Patience continued to watch Tyric as he stood around talking and laughing with V-Chip. She pulled out her cell phone and sent him a text message. She kept her eyes on him as he pulled out his cell phone and read her message. A smile instantly appeared on his face as he looked around the parking lot. Once he spotted her vehicle he said something to V-Chip before slowly making his way over to her car. V-Chip climbed inside their undercover SUV and reclined the seat as he waited for Tyric.

Patience rolled down her window and smiled as Tyric approached her.

"Hello, Officer James," she greeted him in a teasing tone of voice.

"Hey, babe," he greeted her as he tucked his cell phone back on his waistband.

"Where's V-Chip going?" she asked.

Tyric looked back across the street at his partner and said, "Nowhere. He's waiting for me."

She lowered her head and said, "I see."

"What's going on with you? You seem a little sad."

"I'm good," she answered with a lie. The thought of being separated from him saddened her so the need to see him was extra strong.

"That was a nasty text message you just sent me. I thought I warned you about teasing me."

"I'm not teasing you, Tyric. I meant every word I said," she answered with confidence as she made eye contact with him, "I'm just trying to keep you on your toes."

He glanced down at her rose-colored lips and asked, "Is that right?"

Patience nodded and then blushed.

"Well, not really keep you on your toes, but I thought it would at least put a smile on your face."

He chuckled and leaned down in the window until their faces were inches apart.

"It did more than put a smile on my face, but I'll leave that alone for now. Now, may I have a kiss?" he asked.

"I haven't seen or heard from you in two days and now you want a kiss?" she asked. "I don't think so."

Tyric laughed.

"You know it turns me on when you play hard like this. I don't think you know what you do to me. You drive me crazy, Miss Baxter."

She blushed. "You're so silly."

"Am I lying?" he asked.

"Whatever, Tyric," she answered sarcastically.

"You know I speak the truth."

She rolled her eyes and said, "Get over yourself, Tyric."

He laughed because he knew that Patience was trying to minimize the overpowering effect he had on her. The fact was that Tyric knew exactly how to set Patience's mind, body, and soul on fire and the feeling was mutual.

"Hmm, you smell so good," he pointed out as he

stroked her cheek with his finger. "What's that scent?"

"It's Amber Romance by Victoria's Secret."

Tyric inhaled her scent deeper and then planted a butterfly kiss on the curve of her neck.

"Well, I love it, on you."

Patience shivered at the subtle contact of his warm lips on her soft skin.

"Thank you," she whispered.

"You're welcome. Now, what brings you all the way over here?"

"I told you. I haven't seen you in a couple of days."

"I'm sorry. I've been working nonstop since you left my house."

She took his hand into hers and said, "I thought I would get a call, text or something."

Tyric often worked for days at a time, often losing track of time but Patience was never far off his mind. When he was on the streets he couldn't have any distractions and contacting her when he was working the streets often made his mind wander and he couldn't afford making any mistakes. The fact was that he was in love with her and hearing her voice or seeing her face helped him forget all the terrible things he had to deal with on the streets.

"You're right and I'm sorry," he apologized. "Can you forgive me?"

Patience nodded without speaking.

"Thank you. Now I have some good news for you."

"What?"

"I found out who Selena's boyfriend is," he revealed.

Patience's eyes lit up upon hearing the news. "Who is he?"

"His name is Barrington Miller and he lives out in the Piedmont area. He's a couple of years older than your mother, divorced with two college-aged children, no criminal record. He seems to be about as clean as a man can be."

"Piedmont is a nice area. For him to live out there he has to have a good job. Right?" Patience asked. "You know I don't want Momma dating a deadbeat."

Tyric laughed.

"Yeah, he has a job, all right. In fact, he has a great job. He's a bank manager."

"A bank manager? I wonder how they met?"

"Selena works around all those lawyers. She could've met him through them or on her own, but everything I found out about him says he's a stand-up guy."

Patience felt a little better knowing that her mother's new boyfriend seemed to meet Tyric's approval but he had yet to past her scrutiny. Bank manager or not, her mother's happiness was the most important thing to her and time would tell if he would meet her approval.

"Stop worrying about your mom. She's a big girl. She's not going to waste her time on some idiot," Tyric said to try and reassure his lover. Then he switched gears to get her mind off her mother. "How's Jasmine? Is she behaving?"

She shrugged her shoulders. "Jazz is Jazz. She's been cool lately and I haven't seen her hanging around Red Rum so whatever you said to her seemed to have gotten through to her."

Tyric studied her body language. He knew she was being evasive about something but he didn't know what it was.

"What's going on with you, Brianna? I haven't seen you this distracted in a while. Is there something you want to talk about before I leave?"

Patience wanted to talk to him about clearing Shawn's name but she was nervous. She never told him about Pit Bull threatening her life and there was no telling what he might do once he found out.

"No, you have to get to work and I really need to head home."

Tyric walked around to the passenger side of her car and climbed in.

"When are you going to tell me the truth?" he asked.

She wrapped her arms around his neck and buried her face against his warm neck.

He softly caressed her back and whispered, "Talk to me, baby."

She brushed her lips against his and whispered, "What's going to happen to us when I leave for college?"

Seeing Patience's tears hurt Tyric's heart. She wiped her tears away with her hands. She didn't show her soft side often and when she did it was usually only around Tyric or her mother.

"Nothing's going to happen to us as far as I'm concerned. What are you so worried about?"

"We're going to be hundreds of miles apart and I'm worried that I'm going to lose you to somebody else."

He took her hand into his and kissed the back of it. "You're not going to lose me, Brianna. We'll be fine, you'll see."

Patience pulled her hand away.

"Are you saying that you're not going to hook up with someone else while I'm gone?"

He kissed her cheek and said, "What I'm saying is if I'm weak enough to cheat on you while you're at Spelman, I'm man enough to end our relationship before you leave. Brianna, you're where my heart is and if anybody should be worried, it's me. You're going to be around all those rich guys at Morehouse and all those wealthy athletes and musicians living in Atlanta."

"You know I don't care about money."

"Then stop creating drama that's not even there. I love you, Brianna and I know you love me, so it means we have to trust each other."

"Just the thought of another chick rubbing up against you makes me crazy."

Tyric was starting to get frustrated with their conversation and all types of unpleasant visions were running through his head. Now that he'd said it out loud, he had to admit to himself that Patience's beauty was going to be a huge attraction to the college guys. This was the first time they really had a chance to discuss their upcoming separation but he had hoped the transition would be a little easier than she was making it.

"Sweetheart, this is not going to be easy for me either, but I have faith in what we have."

"I know, but I can't help but be worried about us."

He touched her chin with his finger and turned her face to his.

"Do you love me?"

Patience looked over at him and said, "You know I do."

"No, I mean really, really, love me?" he asked.

Tears spilled out of her eyes.

"Yes, Tyric. I love you."

He kissed her smooth lips and then softly said, "Then I have nothing to worry about and neither do you, because I feel exactly the same way about you. We're going to see each other more than you think. You might even get sick of me showing up in Atlanta."

Patience kissed Tyric until she was breathless. "I'll never get sick of you, Tyric. Now, get out of my car and go to work."

"Hold up! How are you going to lay a kiss on me like that and then kick me out of your car?" he teased. "You're going to get me started."

"It has been two days, Tyric. How do you expect me to kiss you?" she joked back.

Tyric quickly opened her car door and let out a breath.

"You're killing me, Brianna."

She gave him one last peck on the lips and said, "You can pay me back later. Now go."

Before walking away, Tyric reached inside his pocket and pulled out a pair of keys and placed them in Patience's hand.

"These are the keys to my house. I want you to have a set."

"Really?" she asked.

"You're my girl, Brianna. I should've given them to you a long time ago. You look like you could use some quiet time so why don't you go on over to my house and chill, sleep, study or whatever. I'll swing by later to check on you."

She climbed out of her car and hugged Tyric's neck. "Thank you, baby."

"You're welcome," he replied as he rested his hands on her hips. "You know you have the most beautiful lips."

"Go to work, Tyric," Patience ordered him playfully as she pushed him away. "I'll probably see you later."

He opened the car door for her so she could climb inside.

"I'm counting on it," he replied before he jogged across the parking lot and climbed into the unmarked vehicle with his partner.

Patience drove through town with Tyric heavy on her mind. She was thankful everyday that God had brought him into her life. He kept her grounded and she trusted him with her life. That's why she felt that now was the best time to tell him about Pit Bull's threat. Even though Shawn was dead she knew the truth and he would never let her rest. As far as her mother and her new boyfriend, well, she hoped she would get to meet him soon because she wouldn't be able to go off to college until she had a chance to check him out.

Chapter Eight

"What do you mean, you missed your period?" Patrice asked.

"Don't make me repeat it," Denim pleaded. "I'm late and I'm never late."

Patrice sat on the sofa and pulled a pillow into her lap. As she hugged the pillow she watched Denim pacing back and forth in front of her.

"Denim, how did you let this happen? You of all people said this could never happen to you. Are you still on the pill?"

She sat down beside Patrice and covered her face with her hands. The thought of having Dré's child was a dream of hers, but not now. They had a plan that included graduating from high school, then college, and then they could get married and have a family. A baby now would put her life right where Patrice's was . . . on pause.

"Yes, and I never miss taking it," she explained, "You know latex is not a hundred percent."

Patrice touched her friend's arm to comfort her. She could hear the fear in her voice and see the stress in her body language. She'd been in her shoes and it was scary.

"Denim, have you and Dré ever got carried away and . . ."

Denim knew exactly what Patrice was asking her. They were close like that and often finished each other's thoughts and sentences. Therefore, before Patrice could get the last words out of her mouth, Denim answered, "Once. We were only together once, unprotected."

"That's all it takes, girl."

Denim shook her head in disbelief and she remembered the night she had cheered Langley High's basketball team to a district championship. They had celebrated with classmates at a school dance afterward but after a few dances they took the celebration to Dré's house, where they watched a movie while eating Italian sub sandwiches and chips. Opportunity presented itself: Dré's parents went out to a jazz club after his game. This gave the teens free reign of the house and opened the door for a sensual tryst, which caused both of them to lose control of their emotions and senses.

"I'm sure you're okay. Just try not to stress over it."

"Easy for you to say. You know how my parents are," Denim reminded her. "They're going to kill me, bury me, dig me up and then kill me again."

"No, they're not. Well, they might hurt you, but not kill you," Patrice joked to try and lighten her friend's mood.

"It's not funny," Denim replied as she walked over to the window and looked outside. Tears were stinging her eyes but she fought back the urge to cry. Patrice joined her at the window and reached into her pocket and pulled out a pack of gum, offering her some.

Denim waved her off.

Patrice stuck a stick of gum in her mouth and asked, "Have you told Dré?"

Denim said, "No, and I don't want to tell him until I know what's up."

Patrice understood Denim's fear and it was very real. First there was the fear of telling the guy, then came the fear of telling your parents. Other fears that took control of your mind was the fear of becoming a parent at such a young age. Reality had a way of slapping you in the face, especially when you realized you had a tiny human being that you were instantly responsible for.

Patrice sat back down and picked up the remote control and turned on the TV. She glanced over at Denim and asked, "Do you want to find out now?"

She wiped away the tears stinging her eyes and turned to Patrice.

"I don't know what I want to do. My stomach is in knots and I have a migraine just thinking about it," she explained. "I mean, I want to know, but then again, I don't want to know."

With a smile on her face, Patrice said, "I have a leftover pregnancy test in my bathroom if you want to use it. You'll know in a few minutes."

Denim's heart leaped in her chest at the thought. If she agreed, her future would be determined by the contents of a box costing only fifteen dollars. It was either stay stressed-out and wonder about the future or man up and face the unknown.

"What if it's positive? Then what?" Denim asked.

Patrice blew a bubble with her gum. After it popped she said, "If it's positive, you'll tell Dré first and then your parents. After that, you'll just deal

with it and I'll help you in any way I can. **Agreed?**"
she asked as she held out her fist for Denim to
bump it.

"Okay," Denim replied as she bumped her fist
against her friend's. "Let's do it."

While Denim waited to find out which road in
life she was about to travel, she pulled her diary
out of her book bag and jotted down her thoughts.

>   *Dear Diary,*
>   *In a few minutes, I'll find out the fate of*
> *my life. My period is four days late and I'm*
> *afraid I'm pregnant. This is not something*
> *we planned but for most kids my age it never*
> *is. I never in my wildest dreams thought it*
> *could happen to me. Lord, please guide my*
> *steps because my parents will kill me if I am*
> *pregnant. I'm so nervous I feel like my heart*
> *is about to burst out of my chest*
>   *Later,*
>   *D*

Thirty minutes later, Denim sobbed in Patrice's
friendly embrace.

"See, I told you everything would be okay. It's

negative," Patrice announced as she held the stick out for her to view again.

Denim wiped away her tears of joy as she stared at the stick in disbelief. Relief swept over her body and the tension in her body that had held her hostage over the past four days had finally eased up. Her stomach was still in knots but the pain in her head was starting to let up until the doorbell rang, interrupting the two.

"Are you expecting someone?" Denim asked as she did her best to wipe the remnants of her tears off her face.

"No," Patrice replied as she looked out the peephole. "Shoot! It's Dré. Get yourself together."

Denim ran into the bathroom to throw some cold water on her face while Patrice opened the door.

"What are you doing here?" she asked with her hands on her hips.

"I came to see my baby," Dré answered with a grin as he stepped through the door.

Patrice closed the door and asked, "Who? Alejandro or Denim?"

Dré turned to Patrice and said, "I see you have jokes."

Patrice laughed and then gave Dré a brotherly hug.

"I know you're here to see Denim but Alejandro would like to see you too."

Dré smiled and said, "One at a time, sis. Let me get some sugar from my baby first."

Dré kissed Denim lovingly as she walked out of the bathroom and into his arms.

"Hey, prime time. What are you doing here?"

"I just thought I would come by to see what you guys were up to."

"You don't have practice today?" Denim asked as she sat back down on the sofa.

"Not today," he answered.

The room was silent for the next few seconds. Dré looked at Patrice and then over at Denim. He got the feeling that something was going on between the two women, but he had no idea what it was.

"What's going on in here? You guys are looking really guilty."

Denim smiled without responding, but Dré could see that he had interrupted something.

"We're just hanging out doing girl talk, that's all. How did you know I was here?"

He caressed her arm and said, "You're always over here."

"I guess I'm busted," she replied.

He turned his attention to Patrice and asked, "What time is DeMario getting off work?"

She looked at her watch and said, "He'll get off in a couple of hours."

"A'ight. What's this?" he asked as he picked up the plastic stick.

Dré looked down on the coffee table and spotted some incriminating evidence. Denim and Patrice had forgotten to throw away the pregnancy-test stick before Dré came in the house. Denim stopped breathing when Dré picked up the stick and looked at it. Patrice's eyes widened and she quickly snatched it out of his hands.

"That's mine, nosy."

"Yours? Don't you think that you and DeMario need to slow down?"

Denim picked up the remote control and immediately started changing the channels on the TV.

Patrice pointed her finger at Dré and threatened him.

"Shut up, Dré, and don't go running your mouth to DeMario."

He sat down on the sofa and said, "Well, let's see. He's my best friend and you're keeping secrets from him. Sounds like I need to have a talk with him again."

"Stop teasing her, Dré, and don't be telling De-Mario anything."

"Why shouldn't I?" he asked.

"Because it's none of your business and if you say anything you'll have to answer to me," she replied.

Dré looked at Denim and saw the expression on her face, which told him she was serious. He put his hands up in defense and said, "Okay! Okay! You don't have to threaten a brotha."

"Nobody's threatening you with your big head. You guys gossip more than we do," Patrice pointed out. "I'm not playing, Dré, keep your mouth shut or you won't have just Denim hitting you upside the head."

Dré stood and said, "I don't have to take all this hostility. I'm going to see my man, Alejandro."

Patrice and Denim watched as Dré left the room to go see Patrice's son. Once he was out of the room, Denim whispered, "That was close. Thanks for saving my butt. I froze like a deer in headlights. I couldn't think of anything to say."

"I knew you would freeze up, that's why I spoke up first. Denim, you need to relax. You're going to give yourself away. You saw how Dré sensed that something was up when he first walked in. Cheer up and stop tripping. Everything turned out fine, so stop stressing."

"I'm trying, Patrice, but I'm still a little shook-up."

Patrice twirled the pregnancy stick through her fingers like it was a baton.

"Denim, what you need to understand is that this scare had nothing to do with the precautions you guys are taking, but it has everything to do with the stress you're under. You're studying for your ACT test and you're working. Is something else going on that you're not telling me?" Patrice asked.

"Well, since I warned Patience about some of those B.G.R. girls, things have been a little crazy. After school the other day a couple of them tried to jump me."

"You better be glad I wasn't with you because it would've been on like popcorn. Girls like that get on my nerves," Patrice acknowledged.

"And you would've been suspended from school too," Denim reminded her.

"Whatever! So what happened?" Patrice asked as she sat Indian-style on the sofa.

"Okay, just when it looked like I was going to have to fight three of those girls, Patience stepped through the crowd and made them go on about their business. Those girls were so pissed at Patience."

"Really? You'd better be glad that Patience is cool with you, otherwise I might be visiting your tail in the hospital."

Denim traced her finger in the floral design on the sofa. Realizing how close she came to getting a real beat-down unnerved her.

"Yeah, I know."

"What happened after Patience broke things up?" Patrice asked.

"I pulled Patience to the side and told her I recognized two of the girls' voices as the ones who was in the deli talking about setting her up."

"You're lying!" Patrice yelled as she slapped her hand down on the sofa.

Denim shook her head and said, "No, it's the truth."

"Did Patience say what she was going to do?"

"No, she just said she would handle it."

Dré walked into the room holding Alejandro, who had the cutest smile on his face. It was obvious he was enjoying the attention from Dré.

"Patrice, I think Alejandro needs a diaper change."

"Can you take care of it?" she asked. "I'm hanging with my girl but if you can't handle it, bring him to me and I'll do it."

"Nah, I got it," he replied.

"Thanks, Dré. Call me if you need me."

Dré held Alejandro up to his face and blew on his stomach, making a loud trumpet noise, and every time Dré did it Alejandro giggled loudly in response.

"Stop spitting on my baby, Dré."

Denim stood and took the pregnancy stick out of Patrice's hand.

"Give that to me before DeMario or your momma finds it and has a heart attack."

Denim dropped it down in her purse. Her plan was to throw it in a dumpster on the way home so nobody would find it and get the wrong impression. About that time, Dré ran into the room and quickly handed Alejandro to Patrice. The diaper was hanging off his bottom and he had powder on him from head to toe. Denim laughed as soon as she saw him because she knew exactly what had happened.

"What did you do to my baby, Dré?" Patrice

yelled as she quickly stood and took Alejandro out of Dré's hands.

Dré turned toward the bathroom and said, "I didn't do anything to him. He peed in my face!"

Patrice laid her son down on the sofa and finished fastening his diaper.

"I thought you said you were going to take care of him, Dré," she yelled out to him.

"I was taking care of him until he peed in my face!" Dré yelled back. The two girls could hear water running from the faucet at full force.

Denim giggled and stood. As she walked across the room toward the bathroom, she looked over at Patrice, who was snapping Alejandro's onesie back together.

"Let me go check on the big baby."

When Denim entered the bathroom she found Dré bent over in the sink, vigorously scrubbing his face. She pulled a towel off the rack and held it out to him.

"You're so sad, Dré. It's only a little baby pee."

He reached for the towel and wiped his face.

"That stuff is lethal," he joked. "He almost got my mouth."

Denim laughed and said, "I didn't know you were such a big baby, Dré."

He reached over her head and pushed the bathroom door closed, leaving them alone in the bathroom.

"Are you pregnant?" he asked, catching her totally off guard.

Denim's eyes widened in shock as Dré looked her directly in the eyes and waited for an answer. She tried several times to speak but when she opened her mouth, nothing would come out.

"Oh, you don't think I'm smart enough to pick up on what you and Patrice were doing?" he asked.

Denim tried her best to swallow the lump in her throat as Dré threw the towel in a nearby hamper and stared with his face within inches of hers. He asked again. "Denim, are you pregnant? And don't lie."

"I—I . . . Dré," she stuttered. It should've been easy for her to answer him, but it wasn't. She felt cornered in the small bathroom with him in her face. She wasn't prepared to discuss the situation with him right now. She'd barely had time to absorb the results herself.

Dré's heart was pounding in his chest as he waited to get a clear response out of her. The possibility of fatherhood was hanging over his head and it was mind-numbing and scary.

She finally cleared her throat and was able to speak. "No, I'm not pregnant."

He towered over her and asked, "Are you serious?"

"Yes, I'm serious," she confirmed softly. "I'm so sorry, Dré. I know I should've told you, but I was so scared."

He leaned against the wall and closed his eyes. "I'm hurt that you felt like you couldn't tell me about it and then you get your girl to cover for you."

Denim's heart ached, knowing that she had disappointed the love of her life. She'd made a mistake and now all that mattered was that he forgave her and that he still loved her.

"I thought we agreed there would be no more secrets between us?"

"I didn't want you to freak out. I would've told you if it had been positive, but it wasn't," she replied as she wrapped her arms around his waist.

The warmth of her body was beginning to soothe him, but he was still upset that she had concealed something so important from him.

She buried her face against his chest and said, "The only reason I took the test in the first place is because I'm running a few days late. Patrice had a kit here so I went ahead and did it. You can't believe I would keep something like that from you if it had been positive."

His pain was starting to melt away as he slowly reached up and caressed her back.

"That's cool, and I know you and Patrice are friends, but I should've been the first to know."

She kissed his chin lovingly and said, "At the time I wasn't thinking and all I wanted to do was to know where we stood. Can you ever forgive me?"

How could he not forgive her? She was his girl and was one of the most important people in his life.

"Of course I forgive you," he revealed as he kissed her forehead. "Just make sure you don't hide anything like that from me again. Okay?"

She tightened her grip around his waist and said, "Without a doubt."

Dré held onto Denim in silence for a while. The bridge they nearly crossed together would've been life-altering for the both of them. If the results had been the opposite, he would've lived up to his responsibilities and taken care of Denim and his child to the best of his abilities. Luckily God and luck were on their side and he never wanted to be in this predicament again.

At that moment, Patrice beat on the door with her fist. "What are you guys doing in there? Is everything okay?"

Dré opened the door and found Patrice standing there with Alejandro in her arms. He allowed Denim to walk out ahead of him and they all made their way back into the family room.

"I know the truth about the pregnancy test," he announced to Patrice. "It's wrong for girls to keep something like that from a dude."

"Whatever, Dré," Patrice replied as she patted Alejandro's back. "Guys don't know what we go through. Denim was scared and we did what we thought was best."

"I don't want to talk about it anymore, so can we just drop it?" Denim asked as she sat next to Dré on the sofa. She was still a little jittery from the whole incident and just wanted to move on.

"Cool with me," Dré answered as he pulled Denim into his lap and turned the TV on ESPN.

"Me too," Patrice also responded and she rocked Alejandro to sleep.

Seconds later, Denim's cell phone rang, revealing an unfamiliar number.

"Hello?"

"Hey, Mitchell, it's Patience. We need to talk."

"This is really not a good time," Denim replied.

Most things didn't distract Dré from ESPN but there was something about her conversation that grabbed his attention. It didn't sound like a casual conversation; he could hear a little tension in her voice.

"Can't it wait until we get to school tomorrow?" Denim asked.

"No, it can't wait. I'll see you in fifteen minutes," Patience replied before hanging up.

Denim slid out of Dré's lap and dropped her cell phone into her purse. She grabbed her keys and said, "I have to go meet somebody."

"It's almost dark outside. Who are you meeting?" Dré asked curiously as he also stood. Denim wasn't normally secretive but for some reason she seemed to be holding back from him.

As she walked toward the door she turned and said, "I'm going to meet Patience."

Chapter Nine

"You're crazy if you think I'm going to let you walk out of here and meet Patience alone."

Denim opened the front door and said, "You don't have to go. Patience is cool. She's not going to hurt me."

Dré picked up his keys, totally ignoring her. "You're not meeting Patience by yourself, end of discussion. Now, let's go so you can get this over with."

Patrice stood in the doorway and watched as Denim and Dré backed out of her driveway.

Nearly ten minutes later, Denim pulled into the Langley High School parking lot and immediately spotted Patience's car.

"There she is," Dré pointed out. "Is she alone?"

"I can't tell," Denim answered as she pulled in beside her.

Patience got out of her vehicle and waved at the couple.

"Hey, Patience," Denim greeted her. "What do you need to talk to me about?"

Before answering her, she looked over at Dré and jokingly said, "I see you brought your bodyguard with you."

Dré took a defensive stance and said, "I see you have jokes. You know I'm not going to let my baby go anywhere by herself where she could get hurt."

Denim interrupted Dré and said, "It's okay, Dré, I got this."

Patience sat on the hood of her car and said, "Calm down, Dré. Listen, Denim, all I need you to do is to have a conversation with Desireé and Kayla and get them to trust you."

Denim looked at Patience, not sure if she heard her correctly. Surely she didn't want her to talk to those two maniacs. They already wanted her head on a platter after their altercation. The less she had to do with them the better.

"You have got to be kidding," Denim responded.

"Yeah, Patience, there's no way they will want to have anything to do with Denim."

"Believe me, they'll trust you, especially after I set the perfect plan in motion with Dré."

"Who, me?" he asked. "How do I play into this?"

Hearing his name immediately got his attention. He was only here to watch over Denim. Getting involved in some female drama wasn't on his agenda.

"Yes, Mr. Basketball, you," Patience revealed. "I thought you were here to help."

Denim rubbed Dré's chest to soothe him. "Let's hear her out, babe."

Patience laid out her plan to Denim and Dré. Everything she said seemed possible but there was one particular part of the plan that Denim wasn't exactly cool with. When she finished explaining everything to them, Denim and Dré looked at each other and searched for some type of confirmation from the other.

"So are you guys game or not?" Patience asked the couple.

Denim gnawed on her nail and said, "I don't know about putting Dré in the mix. Can't you think of something else to do that wouldn't involve him?"

Patience put her hands on her hips and said,

"No, I can't. Listen, Denim, the beauty of it is that Kayla and Desireé won't be expecting any of this. I'm going to need both of you to keep your cool and to be great actors. Once they let their guard down they'll be all mine. Doing anything else will make them suspicious."

"This is crazy," Dré replied.

"Everything will be fine," Patience assured them. "I'm moving to Georgia after graduation and I don't know when I'll be back. I can't leave town without putting an end to this. I need to know why they're after me."

Denim had offered to help Patience from the very beginning, but after her run-in with the two girls she felt like they were hungry for revenge and wouldn't hesitate to get it the first chance they could.

"Let's go!" Dré said as he pulled Denim by the arm over to the passenger-side door of her car.

Not convinced, he turned to Patience and said, "You'll be safely tucked away in college and Denim will still be here to face those girls everyday. You're going to have to find another way that don't involve us."

"Dré, she'll be fine and after this is over, Desireé and Kayla won't have the nerve to even look Denim's way," Patience announced calmly.

Nobody knew her crew like she knew them and there was something about Patience's tone of voice that convinced Denim that she was in good hands. Unfortunately, Dré wasn't so persuaded. In fact, he was still trying to shove Denim into the car so they could leave. If you asked him, her plan was still a little shaky.

"I'll do it," Denim announced as she closed the car door and walked back over to Patience.

"Denim!" Dré yelled in disbelief. He was completely against her decision but could see she was determined to go through with the plan.

"Hold on, baby," Denim stated. "I started this thing so I'm going to finish it. I know what I'm doing, baby, trust me."

Patience smiled and put her hand on Dré's shoulder and said, "Dré, I promise I won't let anything happen to Denim."

He stepped to Patience and sternly said, "You better know what you're doing because if anything—and I mean *anything*—happens to Denim, I promise that you'll have to answer to me. Do you feel me?"

"I feel you," Patience answered.

Denim turned to Dré and took both of his hands

into hers. "I really need you to have my back on this."

Dré let out a breath and pulled her into his arms. "I have to help you because I'm not going to let you do this by yourself."

"Does that mean you're going to help me?" Denim asked as she looked up into his eyes.

He hesitated and then said, "Yeah, babe, I'm going to help you."

"Cool," Patience replied as she clapped her hands together.

Over the next few minutes, Patience instructed them to keep their meeting and the plan secret, because if Desireé or Kayla got any hint that Patience was on to them, the ruse was over before it got started.

Several miles away, Jasmine stood in the alley with Red Rum. It was a narrow alley that ran between the Scotland Heights grocery store and the Wings, Fish and Mo' restaurant. The restaurant was a known hangout for Red Rum and his crew and on any given day they could be found there, shooting dice, eating or conducting some of their illegal activities. Jasmine took the envelope out of

Red Rum's hand and asked, "Who do you want me to give this to?"

"His name is Bombay and you'll know him because he has a mouthful of gold and drives a gold Escalade."

Jasmine tried to take a peek inside the envelope but Red Rum grabbed her wrist, stopping her.

She cuddled up to him and asked, "What do I get for doing this favor for you?"

Red Rum backed her against the wall and pushed his body against hers.

"I have your reward right here," he replied before kissing her neck.

She twisted her mouth and said, "I can get this anytime I want to. I'm talking about real payment."

He stepped back, reached into his pocket and pulled out a wad of money. Jazz's eyes widened as he counted out a couple of bills.

"You chicks are all alike."

Jasmine held out her hand and said, "Whatever. You like it, now pay me because I don't do anything free."

Red Rum placed two one-hundred-dollar bills in her hand and then playfully smacked her on the backside.

"You're a trip, Jazz, but I like that about you."

"I know," she replied as she slid the money into her pocket.

Red Rum put his arm around Jazz and walked around to the front of the store. He looked at his cell phone and said, "We have to go. Bombay will be at the meeting point in ten minutes."

She walked toward his car and opened the car door. Once inside the car she looked over at him. He was cool, calm, and collected but she was starting to get a nervous stomach.

"And all I have to do is give him this envelope?"

Red Rum turned the key in the ignition and said, "Yeah, baby, that's all, now let's go."

He put the car in drive and then quickly pulled out into the traffic and disappeared down the street. As he drove through town, he blasted the radio and bobbed his head when a song by the rapper Ludacris came over the radio. Five minutes later he pulled into the entrance of the city park. Minutes later a gold Escalade pulled up and parked on the other side of the man-made duck pond and slowly made its way to a more secluded section of the park.

"Right on time," Red Rum announced as he smiled, showing his gold tooth that had an ace of spades on it.

"Is that him?" Jazz asked as she squinted her eyes to get a better view of the vehicle.

"Yeah, that's him, so get going."

With the envelope safely tucked in her pocket, she opened the car door and stepped out onto the pavement. She wanted to make Red Rum happy by doing him this favor but her stomach fluttered again, giving away her nervousness. Before walking off, she leaned back into the car and for reassurance asked again, "All I have to do is give him the envelope, right?"

With a frustrated tone of voice, he answered, "Dang, girl, I said that's all. What's up with you?"

She closed the car door and said, "Never mind, I'm cool."

Jazz slowly made her way across the grass to Bombay's waiting car. When she reached the Escalade, the window rolled down on the passenger side and a cloud of smoke drifted out the window. As she looked through the window, she saw a large, dark-skinned black man with even darker sunglasses sitting on the front passenger side. He smiled, showing her a mouthful of gold teeth as the vehicle vibrated from the sound of the music. Two other men sat in the backseat and all eyes, including the driver's, were on her.

"You Red Rum's girl?" the large man in the passenger seat asked with a silly grin on his face.

Without answering his question, she asked one of her own.

"What's your name?"

He laughed out loud and so did the other men in the vehicle.

"You have questions for me, but you won't answer mine?"

"I'm not here for conversation," she replied in a sassy tone. "But I need to know your name before we do this."

All Jazz wanted to do was get this over with so she could leave. She was uncomfortable and felt vulnerable with God-knows-what in the envelope.

"Damn, girl! Everybody knows I'm Bombay! Now do you have something for me or not?"

Jazz frowned and stared harder at the large, obnoxious man but before she could hand him the envelope he swung open the car door, nearly knocking her down. He grabbed her by the arm and yelled, "I don't have time for this! What you got for me?"

He cornered her against the vehicle, blocking her from Red Rum's view. Jazz tried to step around him but he blocked her from leaving, causing her to go into a slight panic. That's when Bombay twisted her arm behind her back.

"You're hurting me!" she yelled out in pain.

"I don't care. Where's my stuff?" he asked as he ran his hands all over her body.

"Turn me loose!" she yelled as she struggled to free herself.

Bombay grabbed her by the collar and pulled her close to his face. "The next time I ask you a question, you'd better answer me. Do you understand?"

"Yes," Jazz struggled to get the answer out of her mouth as the burning sensation from the pain radiated all over her body.

Bombay released her and then patted her down. He found the envelope in her back pocket and shoved her onto the ground after snatching it away from her. Jazz fell hard on her backside and when she fell, all the men in the car burst out laughing. When Bombay climbed back inside the vehicle, he looked over at the driver and said, "Let's roll, man,"

This angered Jazz so she cursed loudly at Bombay and before they got six feet she picked up a large rock and threw it at the Escalade. The sound was deafening as the rock hit the back window of the vehicle. Bombay yelled an obscenity when he realized that Jazz had cracked the window. The Escalade came to a screeching halt and one of the men from the backseat quickly jumped out of the car and picked up Jazz before she could run. He threw her in the backseat, causing Jazz to kick and scream as the vehicle sped off toward the exit. Red Rum saw what was happening and knew he was about to commit suicide by blocking their path, but he couldn't let Bombay snatch his girl. The gold Escalade neared the exit with Red Rum following close behind them. Just then, two undercover police vehicles blocked the exit and several officers jumped out with guns drawn on both vehicles.

"Get on the ground!" they yelled repeatedly as they pulled the men one by one out of the SUV and onto the ground

Red Rum put his vehicle in reverse and tried to speed out another exit but was apprehended by two police cruisers. He put his hands up and voluntarily laid on the ground. Once all the perpetrators were on the ground, Jazz was quickly escorted to the safety of one of the police cruisers

"Are you okay?" one of the narcotics officers asked Jazz.

She nodded that she was okay as she wiped

stray tears off her cheeks. Her tan jeans and teal T-shirt were soiled with dirt and grass from being shoved to the ground by Bombay.

"What's your name?" the officer asked.

"Jasmine Baxter," she answered through her sobs.

The officer jotted Jasmine's name down on a notepad and then asked, "How old are you?"

Jasmine looked up at him and said, "I'm sixteen."

"Are you injured?"

"No, I'm fine. I just have a few scratches and bruises," she answered as she inspected her forearm.

"Do you need me to have a paramedic check you out?"

"No, Officer, I said I was fine."

Then just as the officer was about to ask her another question, Tyric stepped through the crowd. He showed the officers his badge and walked over to where Jazz was sitting.

"Jasmine, what happen? Are you okay?"

Jazz jumped up and hugged Tyric's neck. Among all the chaos, she was relieved to see a familiar face.

"I'm sorry, Tyric. I think I really messed up this time. Momma's going to kill me."

He comforted her as best he could and said, "It's okay, Jasmine. Your mom's not going to kill you. Just be quiet and let me handle this."

The narcotics officer who was questioning Jasmine walked over to where the two were standing.

"Officer James, do you know this young woman?" he asked.

"Yes, she's a close family friend. Her brother was Ryan Baxter."

The officer's head dropped and said, "I didn't know."

The officer turned to Jazz and said, "I'm sorry about your brother, Miss Baxter. The short time I knew him, he was a good man."

"Thank you," she replied softly.

The officer turned back to Tyric.

"Tyric, we have a situation here. Miss Baxter was caught making a transaction with Bombay. You know I have to take her in."

Tyric instructed Jasmine to stay put while he pulled the narcotics officer to the side so they could talk in private.

"From what I heard, Jasmine was called over to the vehicle and assaulted before she was thrown into the backseat. Sounds to me like assault and attempted kidnapping. Did you find anything illegal on her?" Tyric asked.

"No, but our surveillance team said they have her on videotape walking over to the vehicle."

"Does this tape showing her exchanging anything to the perps?" Tyric inquired.

"Not really, but an envelope with a large amount of money and some weed with a small vial of crack cocaine was found in the Escalade. We have to hold her on suspicion of the sale of a controlled substance until we get all of this sorted out."

"Not today. She's a minor and you can't question her outside the presence of her parents or a lawyer. You have no evidence against her, so all it looks like to me is that she was in the wrong place at the wrong time and almost became a victim."

"Come on, James, it's obvious what happened here."

Tyric motioned for Jazz to come over to him. "From where I'm standing there's a lot of circumstantial evidence. Besides, it's about the law and police procedure. The only thing you can question her as is a witness and nothing else."

"Either way, we still need to talk to her," the officer called out to Tyric as he walked Jazz over to his vehicle.

Tyric opened the back door and said, "I'll personally bring her in with her mother tomorrow."

V-Chip turned to Jasmine and shook his head.

"Don't start with me, V-Chip. I know I messed up so you don't have to rub it in."

He threw his hands up in defense and said, "I didn't say a word. I was just going to ask you if you were okay?"

Jasmine nodded without verbally responding.

Tyric pulled a first-aid kit out of the back of the vehicle and tended to her cuts. She cringed when Tyric applied the antibiotic solution to her arms because it stung the open wounds.

"What's going to happen to me?" she asked solemnly.

"Nothing if you do what I tell you," he answered softly. "You know, I am so tired of this thing with you and Red Rum."

"She needs a butt-whipping," V-Chip added as he pulled out his cell phone and started texting someone.

"Not now, bro," Tyric pleaded with V-Chip. "Jasmine, what were you doing?"

"I was giving that guy named Bombay an envelope for Red Rum," she replied as she blew on the scrapes to cool the stinging sensation.

He closed the first-aid kit and asked, "What was inside it?"

"I don't know," she answered.

"Did Bombay give you anything?"

"No, all Red Rum told me to do was give Bombay the envelope."

He closed her door and then climbed into the passenger seat and announced, "There was a large amount of money in the envelope. It was probably payment for Red Rum selling that mess for him. You got lucky this time."

Chapter Ten

The next night, Patience sat in the living room with V-Chip while Tyric filled Selena in on the incident Jasmine was involved in with the police. Patience stared at Tyric as he sat at the kitchen table with her mother while V-Chip played the Xbox. Selena couldn't believe what Tyric was telling her. She had gone to sleep early when Tyric and V-Chip brought Jasmine home the night before and ever since then, she'd noticed that Jasmine was a little distant. Patience could see her mom and Tyric from where she was sitting but she could barely hear what was being said so she eavesdropped the best she could. What she did hear was that Jasmine wasn't going to be charged with any crime; however, she was going to be severely punished. Selena approved Tyric arranging an up-close and personal tour of a women's jail. Secondly, she was to spend two hours working with inner-city kids at the Boys and Girls Club in Scotland Heights after school. She was put on Selena Baxter's house arrest indefinitely and that was just the beginning.

"Stop being so nosy, Brianna," V-Chip ordered her. "You better be glad they're not over there talking about you crawling around under the sheets with Tyric."

"You just play the game, Vernon," she replied with an irritated tone while putting emphasis on his real name. "I'm sorry Tyric ever told you about us."

V-Chip laughed.

"Well, he did and there's nothing you can do about it, sweetheart."

She looked at him curiously.

"You would love to see Momma freak out about us, wouldn't you?"

"No. Besides, why do you think she would freak out?" he asked as he glanced over at her. "She loves Tyric like he was her son. I can't see her going off too much about it but what she will be pissed about is that you've been sneaking."

"He's so much older than me and he was Ryan's best friend."

V-Chip stopped playing the game for a second.

"So what? Do you think Ryan would be upset that you hooked up with him?"

"No," she responded immediately. "He loved Tyric."

"I rest my case," he replied as he picked the Xbox control back up and continued to play the game.

"I hope you're right because I plan on telling Momma about us soon."

He chuckled. "I'm glad, because I don't know how much longer my partner is going to be able to keep it a secret. If you ask me, I think Selena already suspects something's going on between you two."

Patience took the game control out of his hand and quizzed him on what he knew. Before answering, he snatched the game control right back from her and said, "You should see how your face lights up when he's around. If I see it, I'm sure she's noticed it too."

Could V-Chip be right? Did her mother know she was being intimate with Tyric? If so, why hadn't she confronted her about it? The again, maybe V-Chip was blowing hot air just to make her nervous.

"You're full of it, V-Chip. If Momma thought I was creeping with Tyric, she would've said something by now."

"Not necessarily. I said I think she suspects, which means she's probably still gathering evidence against you. Your birthday's coming up, isn't it?"

"Yes," she replied.

"Well, if you're planning on telling her you better make it quick before you get busted."

Patience quietly thought to herself. She didn't want her mother upset with her, but V-Chip did have some valid points. Then again, he was doing a good job making her nervous. Now she didn't know what to believe, but one thing she was sure of was that she had let V-Chip get in her head and it angered her. She reached over and pinched his large bicep.

"Dang, girl! Why did you pinch me? That hurt!" V-Chip jumped up and rubbed the tender area on his arm.

"I meant for it to hurt!" She leaned over and whispered, "That's what you get for messing with my head."

"You need to cut down your claws," he replied as he continued to rub his arm.

Selena looked in the direction of the living room and frowned.

"Brianna, you and Vernon stop fighting."

"He started it, Momma."

V-Chip sat back down and balled his fist up at her.

"I'm going to get you for that."

"You know you're wrong," she whispered. "I should pinch you again."

"You better stay away from me, girl."

"Tyric, get your partner," Selena begged as she stood and put her coffee cup in the sink. "You know you can't leave those two alone for too long."

Tyric walked into the living room, where he found V-Chip and Patience with scowls on their faces.

"Come on, partner, leave Brianna alone. We need to get going anyway."

V-Chip stopped, turned off the Xbox, and stood. "You need to tell her to leave me alone. Did you see what she did to me?" he asked as he pointed at the swollen mark on his arm.

Patience winked at V-Chip and smiled.

Tyric walked over and kissed Patience on the corner of the lips and said, "Stop being mean, Brianna."

Tyric wanted to kiss her square on the mouth but resisted the urge because Selena was in the room.

"You two really need to stop fighting so much. You're like oil and water."

"He started it, Tyric," she replied as she put her hands on her hips. "He always starts it."

"Well, I'm finishing it," Tyric announced. "Jasmine, I'll see you tomorrow after school for our visit to lockup."

The next afternoon, Jazz followed the sheriff through the locked doors of jail. She was on the first of two trips to the area's female correction facility. She couldn't believe the smells, sights, and sounds she was experiencing. The women behind the doors looked like caged animals and some of them were acting like it too as they screamed and yelled out at her. It was horrible and nothing like she envisioned. She'd visited an animal shelter before and the scene was eerily and sadly similar.

"Is it like this all the time?" she asked as they walked through the cement and steel building.

The female sheriff looked over at Jasmine and said, "This is nothing. You should see how they act when they're really worked up."

"Hey, sweet cakes! You sure are pretty," a large

African-American lady yelled at Jazz as she reached out to her through the bars. Another one blew kisses at Jazz and make lewd gestures at her. Whistles and catcalls were hurdled at her the entire time she was in jail. It was a bizarre scene and wasn't a place she ever wanted to go.

"Miss Baxter, as you can see, most of the prisoners are in their cells. They get a little time to exercise and they have work responsibilities. A few of them actually want to do something with their lives after they get out, so they're trying to finish their education. Their days are scheduled and very routine and for some people it makes them a little crazy. This is not a place you want to end up in. If you have a chance to turn your life around, I suggest you do it before you find yourself sleeping next to someone like Crazy Kim," the correction officer said as she pointed into one of the cells. When Jazz saw Crazy Kim she started sweating. She had to have been at least four hundred pounds of mostly muscle. Her hair was cut close to her head and she looked and acted like a man instead of a woman.

"Please, Officer, I'm ready to go," Jazz pleaded with her.

"Not until you see the bathroom."

Jasmine swallowed the lump in her throat and then followed the officer into the large bathroom and shower area.

By the time Tyric picked Jazz up from her tour, she was in tears. Seeing humans with their freedom snatched from them and living like caged animals was too much for her.

He put his arm around her shoulders and escorted her out to his waiting car. Once inside the car, he softly asked, "Are you okay?"

"Not really," she answered through her sobs.

"Now do you understand why I've been working so hard to keep you out of trouble?"

She nodded in silence and wiped away her tears.

"Yes. Tyric, I'm so sorry I've given you such a hard time. I never want to end up in a place like this. It's horrible and the smells . . . all I wanted to do was get out of there."

"The sad thing, Jasmine, is that those women have committed crimes and they can't leave. You've been given a second chance. Make the most of it."

"I will. I promise, just take me home."

Jazz's tour of the women's jail was effective and Tyric got the response he wanted from her. He turned up the air conditioner on his car and drove out of the jail parking lot.

"Tomorrow you start working with the youth at the center. I hope you're serious about changing your life, Jasmine, because if you don't watch it, this is where you're going to end up."

"Thanks for not giving up on me."

He looked over at her and smiled with satisfaction.

"You're like family to me, Jasmine. If I didn't think you were worth saving I wouldn't have wasted my time."

Chapter Eleven

A couple of weeks later Patience's eighteenth birthday had finally arrived and she couldn't have been happier as she walked across the school parking lot with Jasmine. Everything seemed to be coming together in her life so she could concentrate on graduating and leaving Scotland Heights for college. But there was still one little matter left for her to take care of before she left.

Jasmine hurried to catch up with Patience as she made her way toward school. Her grades had improved completely and she enjoyed working with the kids at the youth center. It seemed like she had a new appreciation for life, her family, and for herself.

"Slow down, sis. What's your hurry?" Jasmine asked.

"I don't want to be late."

What Jasmine didn't know was that Patience's mind was consumed with Kayla and Desireé and secondly—and most importantly—she wanted her mother and Jazz to know that Tyric was the love of her life.

"Hold up, sis. I have something for you," Jazz pleaded with her as they got closer to the entrance.

Patience stopped walking and turned to her sister and asked, "What is it, Jazz?"

Jazz pulled a pink card out of her book bag and yelled, "Ta-da! Happy birthday, Patience!"

Patience smiled and took the envelope out of her sister's hand and opened it.

Inside was a very touching card and a hundred-dollar gift card from a local mall.

"This is so cool, Jazz. Thank you."

Jazz smiled with satisfaction, seeing that she had pleased her sister. "So when are we going shopping?"

She slid the birthday card into her book bag and hugged her lovingly. "We can go after school."

"I can't go, remember? I have to go to the youth center," Jazz reminded her.

"Not today. I'm going to call Tyric later and see what he can work out for you. Now come on, we have to get to class."

The bell rang, alerting the pair it was time for first-period class. As she made her way down the hallway, she pulled out her cell phone and sent a text message. Before tucking it away she smiled and mumbled, "Let the games began."

After first-period class Patience found Dré at the water fountain leaning over, getting a drink. When he turned around, he was face-to-face with her.

"Hey, Patience, what's up?"

"This is what's up," she replied before kissing him hard on the lips.

Their kiss drew stares and several classmates pointed in disbelief.

"Dang, girl!" he yelled as he jumped back from her.

Patience wiped the moisture from her lips and said, "Mmm, I've been waiting to do that for a long time. Now I see why Mitchell is so crazy about you."

Dré twitched nervously because he knew enough people saw them kissing for it to get back to Denim.

Patience reached up and cupped his face and said, "I know you liked it and just for the record, there's more where that came from."

He scratched his head and chose his words carefully. Patience was tall, gorgeous, and had curves in all the right places, but Denim was his girl and everybody knew it.

"What the hell is wrong with you?"

Patience snuggled up to him and said, "What I did was something I know you've been dreaming about. Don't front, because you definitely enjoyed it."

"I'm not fronting!"

She winked at him and whispered, "The body doesn't lie and yours told me everything I needed to know."

"You're crazy!" he yelled as he pushed passed Patience. When he looked up he was face-to-face with Denim and by the expression on her face she was livid. Either the news of the kiss had gotten back to her or she'd heard part of his conversation with Patience.

"Denim, baby, I was just coming to find you."

She pointed her finger at him and said, "How can you look for me when your tongue is down Patience's throat? I can't believe you would do something like this to me."

"Denim, she kissed me!" Dré yelled to plead his case.

With hurt in her voice, Denim answered, "I'm not stupid. It takes two."

Patience smiled and said, "Chill, Mitchell. It was just a kiss. I must say your boy has skills, though."

Denim walked over to Patience and got in her face and sprung on her before she could finish her sentence. Her actions startled not only Dré but Patience as well. Before anyone could react, she had Patience by the hair. She slammed her against the lockers, causing everyone in the hallway to scream out in shock.

Dré pulled Denim off Patience right before the resource officer arrived to break up the melee.

"Come on, Denim, before you get kicked out of school."

She pulled away from him angrily and yelled, "Get your hands off me. I hate you!"

"Come on, Denim. Patience kissed me, I didn't kiss her."

Denim reluctantly allowed Dré to pull her down the hallway but before she left she pointed her finger at Patience and threatened the toughest girl in school right in front of a hallway full of students.

"Stay away from Dré or else."

"Or else what, Mitchell?" Patience asked, clearly not worried about Denim's threats. She'd been threatened before by more sinister girls. Dealing with Denim was going to be a no-brainer.

By the time Denim made it to her next class she was furious. It was the beginning of the last six weeks of school and who did she find in her biology class but Kayla, one of the girls who were plotting to set up Patience. She was already sitting at one of the tables so she took a deep breath and sat down without looking at her. Kayla frowned and looked Denim up and down.

"I know you're not going to sit next to me?" she asked.

"I sit anywhere I want to," Denim replied as she sat down next to the young woman. "What's your problem, anyway?"

"My problem is you, Denim Mitchell," she revealed. "I'm so sick of you walking around here like you're better than everyone else with your fancy clothes and souped-up Mustang. You're dating one of the hottest guys in school and then you try to put a wedge between B.G.R. and Patience. What else do you want to know?"

Denim smiled at her and sarcastically replied,

"Is it my fault that my parents work hard to give me nice things? And if you didn't know already, I have a job, so I don't have to ask my parents for everything."

"Whatever! I guess I'd better shut up before Patience runs in here to your rescue."

Denim opened her book and started flipping through the pages. "If you just have to know, Patience and I are not friends anymore."

This bit of information caught Kayla's attention. Patience and Denim had been mysteriously thick as thieves but to find out that was no longer the case made her curious. Kayla sat next to Denim in silence for a few seconds until she decided to take a chance and find out what had caused the two to go their separate ways.

"What happened?" Kayla asked. "It seemed like Patience had turned into your bodyguard or something."

"It's none of your business," Denim replied without making eye contact with her. She continued to flip through the pages of the biology book, looking at the colorful pictures. However, she could still feel Kayla's eyes on her.

"Seriously, what happened between you guys?" Kayla asked again.

Denim slammed the book closed and yelled, "Ask around if you want to know so bad. Better yet, ask Patience. I'm sure she would love to tell you and anyone who'll listen."

"What are you talking about?"

"Just leave me alone! You don't like me and I don't like you, so leave it at that."

Kayla studied Denim curiously. Whatever happened between Denim and Patience had to have been serious and she couldn't wait to find out what it was.

Just then a last bell rang as a few more students filed into the classroom and Kayla noticed they were pointing at Denim. Before she could go over to them, the teacher called the class to order. After she took the roll the instructor grouped the students off for their in-class assignments, which was to go over a series of study questions. Kayla finally found an opportunity to make her way over to the two girls who were pointing at Denim to find out what was going on.

"Why were you guys pointing at Denim Mitchell when you came in?"

One of the girls looked at Kayla and asked, "You didn't hear?"

"Hear what?" Kayla asked.

"Denim caught Patience kissing her man in the hallway and they got in a fight."

Kayla said, "Excuse me? No, you must be mistaken," she told the girls.

"It's the truth," one of the girls explained. "I thought I was dreaming when Denim had Patience against the lockers. If Dré hadn't pulled her off Patience, I don't know what would've happened."

Kayla rejoined her group and sat down in disbelief. She looked across the room at Denim and wondered if she'd had her all wrong. Maybe there was more to her than her or Desireé gave her credit for. If this was the case, looks were definitely deceiving and knowing that Denim jumped Patience in the heat of passion over Dré signaled what could be the beginning of a very interesting situation.

Kayla couldn't wait for class to end. She didn't remember a thing her study group talked about because she was too busy studying Denim. As she sat in class, she was cool for someone who had just fought the head of a gang. Maybe she had a death wish after all or maybe she was crazy. Whatever it was, she was starting to admire her and needed to tell Desireé as soon as possible, but first she needed to talk to Denim just a little bit more. Just then the bell rang and she quickly gathered up her books so she could walk out with Denim.

As they made their way out into the hallway, Kayla said, "I heard that you squared off with Patience over Dré. Is it true?"

"I saw you talking to those girls in class so don't act like you don't know what happened," Denim replied as she put her book bag on her shoulders.

"I know you're pissed. I would be pissed too if another chick kissed my man. I don't blame you for trying to beat Patience down," Kayla revealed as she hit her fist against her open palm.

Denim looked over at Kayla curiously and asked, "I know you're not taking my side against your fearless leader?"

Kayla pulled out a cherry Tootsie Pop and popped it in her mouth. "I'm just saying, I understand what you did."

Denim stopped walking when she got to an intersecting hallway and turned to Kayla. "Look, I don't know why you're following me, but I'd appreciate it if you would leave me alone."

"You know it's not over, right?" Kayla announced.

Denim looked at her with a heated glare. "Do you think I'm worried about that? I told her myself that it wasn't over. She knows I'm going to be coming after her. She just don't know how or when."

"For real?" Kayla said in complete shock.

"When it comes to Dré, I don't play!" Denim yelled. "Now leave me alone!"

Kayla watched as Denim disappeared down the hallway and into the crowd. Just then a lightbulb went off in her head. Maybe this was the break they'd been looking for and it couldn't have come at a more perfect time. With a sly grin on her face, she made her way to her next class and she couldn't wait to see Desireé. Their plan might fall into place quicker than they anticipated.

After school, Kayla filled Desireé in on her conversation with Denim. She had already heard about the altercation with Patience and her mind was already on fast-forward. With Patience distracted by her issues with Denim and upcoming graduation, it would be the opportune time for them to finally make their move. Patience wouldn't know what hit her and Denim just might be the last piece to the puzzle in order for them to get the justice they deserved.

Patience sat in her car waiting for Jasmine to come out of school. When she finally made it over to her, she climbed in on the passenger side and slammed the door.

"Is it true? Did you really kiss Dré?"

Patience laughed and started up the car. "Calm down, sis. It's not what you think. Besides, it was just a kiss. Why is everybody freaking out so hard about it?"

"Why Dré? You've been without a man too long. I could've introduced you to somebody. You don't go after another chick's man. I shouldn't have to tell you that."

Patience pulled out of the student parking lot and into traffic.

"I heard Denim sprung on you."

"She did," Patience admitted as she rubbed her neck. "I guess she had a right to. Look, it was only a kiss. I'm graduating in less than two months, so what if I did do something spontaneous? It's my birthday, so give me a break."

"That don't mean lose your mind." Jazz was so confused over Patience's behavior and why Dré? From what she'd seen over the past few months, Patience and Denim had been close friends. Maybe graduation was making her act crazy or could it be lack of male affection? Whatever it was, she needed to get ahold of herself and fast.

"Enough about me, Jazz. Did Tyric get you the day off from the youth center?"

"Yeah, he told me not to worry about it. He said he was coming by the house later to give you your present."

Patience tried to keep from smiling. She could only imagine what kind of gift he had for her.

"Did he say what he got me?" she asked.

"You know he's not going to tell me anything because he knows I have loose lips," she admitted. "Hey, have you ever wondered why we've never seen Tyric with a girl?"

Patience frowned. The thought of Tyric with another girl made her stomach do a flip.

"No, why do you ask?"

"I just think it's strange. I hope he's not one of those down-low brothas."

Patience hit the brakes hard at the traffic light, causing Jazz to be thrown forward in her seat belt.

"What's wrong with you? You almost killed me!" Jazz yelled."

"Don't ever say that about Tyric again. You know he's not on the down-low. He was Ryan's best friend. You might as well have said Ryan was gay."

Jazz adjusted her seat belt and said, "Dang! Don't get your blood pressure up, sis. I was just talking. Tyric is too cute and fine not to be dating someone. That's all I'm saying."

The light turned green and Patience gripped the steering wheel hard as she drove through the intersection. She didn't appreciate Jazz talking about Tyric even though it was innocent speculation. She nearly lost control with Jazz and almost gave away the fact that she was the mystery woman in Tyric's life. It wouldn't take much for Jazz to figure things out if she didn't keep her cool. Without Red Rum around to keep her occupied, Jazz had more time to keep up with what was going on in her life and with B.G.R.

"Maybe he is dating somebody. He's not required to tell us his business and you don't have to know it, either."

"If you say so," Jazz replied as she pulled out her cell phone and exchanged a series of text messages with a friend.

The next couple of hours the two sisters enjoyed each other's company in an area mall. They tried on expensive clothing they knew they couldn't afford, a ritual they did every time they shopped together. Afterward they made a few purchases of T-shirts, jeans, and earrings to finish off their wonderful afternoon together before heading home.

Chapter Twelve

*W*hen Patience pulled up in the driveway a huge smile appeared on her face as her mother stepped out on the porch.

"Jasmine, make your sister close her eyes before she comes inside."

Patience and Jazz loved birthdays because their mother always turned it into a big celebration with decorations, food, and the whole nine yards. When Patience stepped on the porch she did as she was told and closed her eyes. As Jazz led her through the door, Selena finally gave the okay for her to open her eyes. When she did, she gasped. Standing in the living room next to Selena was Tyric, V-Chip, Nanna, her grandmother on her father's side, her mother's brother, Uncle Tito, and his wife, Aunt Gracie.

"Happy birthday!" they yelled in unison.

Selena kissed her daughter and led her over to a table where a beautiful sheet cake decorated in her favorite colors of lavender and pink sat along with confetti, balloons, party hats, and several beautifully decorated gifts.

V-Chip held a hot wing up to his mouth and winked at Patience.

"Happy birthday, baby girl!"

"Thank you, V-Chip," she replied with her tear-filled eyes.

"Hi, Nanna," Patience said as she hugged and kissed her grandmother on the cheek just before she pulled out a cigar and lit it.

Selena took the cigar out of her hand and said, "Didn't I tell you to stop smoking in the house? You're going to kill yourself with those things," she announced.

"I'm eighty years old, which means I'm grown. If I want to smoke, I'm going to smoke," Nanna replied as she pulled another cigar out of her purse.

Everyone laughed at her comment. Nanna was a feisty woman who looked fifteen years younger than her real age and even though Selena was her daughter-in-law, she loved her as if she was her own child.

"Let her smoke, Momma," Patience pleaded.

"You need to listen to your daughter, Selena."

Patience went on to greet her aunt and uncle and finally made her way back over to her mother. Patience hugged her lovingly and thanked her for throwing her the party.

"You're very welcome, Brianna. I love you so much."

"I love you too, Momma."

Tyric walked over and gave Patience a bear hug, picking her off the floor.

"Happy birthday, sweetheart."

She looked into his eyes and whispered, "Thank you, baby. I love you."

Tyric eased her back down on the floor and smiled. There was something about the way Tyric was looking at her that sent a warm calmness over her body. Patience felt his intense love every time she looked into his eyes and she couldn't go another day without sharing it with the people she loved. Today was the perfect day while everyone was together and she wanted to do it before she lost the nerve so she took Tyric by the hand and called everyone to attention.

"Hey, guys, I want to thank all of you for coming to my party but this won't be complete if I didn't let you in on something that I've been keeping from you for almost a year now."

Tyric gave her hand a gentle squeeze. He realized what she was about to do and wanted to reassure her. This was the moment he'd been waiting for and it was finally here.

Selena looked at her daughter curiously and asked, "What is it, Brianna?"

"Momma, I don't have to tell you how hard it was on all of us after we lost Ryan. I know we all grieved for him in our own way because he was the love of our lives and personally I know I wouldn't have gotten through it if it hadn't been for Tyric."

V-Chip smiled because he was the only one in the room outside of Patience and Tyric who knew exactly where she was going with her speech.

Patience turned to Tyric with tears in her eyes and cupped his face.

"What the—" Jazz mumbled.

"Momma, Jazz, everybody, I want you guys to

know that I haven't been honest with you when it comes to my love life."

"Uh-oh," Nanna mumbled as she puffed on her cigar.

"I knew it!" Jazz yelled out and she started jumping up and down and pointing at the couple.

"What are you screaming about, Jasmine?" Selena asked.

"Momma, I've been dating Tyric for nearly eight months. I love him and I didn't tell you because I didn't know how you would react."

Selena was stunned. Right under her nose her daughter had revealed something she was either too blind to see or was in denial.

"Tyric, you could've told me."

He took Selena by the hands and said, "We didn't know how you would take the news since I'm so much older than Brianna, but I want you to know that I love her and she's the only one for me."

Patience's grandmother blew a smoke circle in the air and said, "You're not that much older than Brianna. Now my third husband, Hubert, he was ten years older than me and baby, let me tell you, that man could—"

"Nanna!" Selena yelled, stopping her mid-sentence. She knew her mother-in-law and had she not stopped her she would've told some type of erotic tale about her marriage in front of everyone.

Selena shook her head in disbelief. She was still trying to absorb the news. It wasn't that she was upset that they were a couple—she was upset that they kept it from her. She sat down in a chair in the living room and put her hands over her face.

"Brianna, I'm hurt that you felt like you couldn't confide in me. I'm your mother, for god's sake."

Nanna walked over to Selena with her plate of food in hand and sat down at the table.

"Selena, get a hold of yourself. You're acting like it's the end of the world. I like the boy. He *was* Ryan's best friend, wasn't he?"

"I agree with Nanna," Tito added. "Tyric's already like family. What's the big deal? I'm hungry, can we eat now?"

"I'm way ahead of you," Nanna replied as she dug into her potato salad.

Selena waved them off and said, "Yes, of course, go ahead and eat."

While everyone else fixed their plates to eat, Tyric held onto Selena's hands as he sat with Selena and Brianna in the family room.

"Selena, we wanted to tell you but we wanted to

wait until we thought the time was right. I love Brianna and you know I would never hurt her."

Selena realized she had been had by her own daughter. Now that she knew that Tyric was the man in her daughter's life she could see how she only saw what she wanted to see in their relationship. She didn't pay any attention to the hugs, the kisses, or the frequent visits to the house. She just chalked them up to him being protective of the girls since Ryan passed away.

"They had a good reason, Selena," Uncle Tito added. "You can be a little extreme with certain things. I grew up with you, remember?"

"Am I that bad?" Selena asked her family members.

"No, Momma, you're not bad at all," Patience said as she hugged her. "I didn't want to disappoint you. That's all."

Selena smiled and held both Tyric's and Patience's hands.

"Then you have my blessings."

"Thank you, Momma."

Selena clapped her hands together and said, "Come on and get some food. I know you're hungry."

Tyric pulled Patience into his arms and kissed

her lovingly. "I'm glad everybody finally knows about us."

With her arms around his neck, she answered, "Me too."

After dinner, Patience opened the rest of her gifts, which included a monogrammed Bible from her grandmother and money, and then gift cards from Uncle Tito and Aunt Gracie. Selena handed her daughter two gifts. One was a pair of diamond earrings that belonged to Patience's maternal grandmother, which had been passed down through the generations and now was Patience's turn. The next gift from her mother was a beautiful birthday card, which held a gift card to her favorite clothing store. Then everyone watched as Tyric pulled out a small box wrapped in pink and lavender paper and handed it to her. Her hands were shaking as she nervously opened the box. He had great taste and she knew that whatever was inside would make her love for him even stronger. As she opened the black velvet box, she screamed and tears flowed down her face. Inside was the gold angel necklace he had noticed her eyeing every time they went past a particular jewelry store. He always felt like Brianna was his angel so the necklace was appropriate and the perfect reminder of how much he really loved her.

Before the night came to an end, Tyric asked Selena if he could take Brianna to Atlanta to see the Spelman campus and tour Atlanta. Selena's eyes swelled with tears, knowing that her daughter had grown into a vibrant young woman of eighteen years old and in love. She realized that she wasn't in charge anymore, but if she had to give up her rank, it couldn't be to a more worthy person. Therefore, she agreed to the trip and gave Tyric her approval.

After all the food was put away and the decorations taken down, Jazz found the opportunity to talk to her sister privately.

"Where's Momma?" Jazz asked.

"She's gone to bed," Patience replied. "I think she has a migraine."

Jazz put the freshly washed dishes in the cabinet and said, "I guess so. I still can't believe you didn't tell me about you guys."

Patience swept up the last of the confetti and said, "You have a big mouth, Jazz. I couldn't risk Momma finding out before I had a chance to tell her."

"Tyric James is a sly devil after all and so are

you. Now I know why you freaked out on me in the car earlier today when I said Tyric might be a down-low brotha."

"You're stupid, Jazz, but you're my sister so I have to love you no matter what."

Jazz sat down on the sofa with a silly grin on her face. Patience looked over at her as she scooped the confetti up in the dustpan.

"Why are you looking at me like that?"

"You know why," Jazz replied as she folded her arms. "I want details."

"You want details about what?" Patience asked as she sat down in the wing-back chair across from Jazz and closed her eyes.

"Now that I know about you and Tyric, I want to know if he is a good kisser or has he used his handcuffs on you? You know, stuff like that."

Patience stood and said, "See, that's exactly why I didn't tell you about us. You take things too far, Jazz."

"I was just kidding," Jazz revealed as she followed her down the hallway and into her room. As she sat on the foot of her sister's bed she said, "You don't have to get all mad."

Patience stuffed a few items into her duffel bag and said, "It's cool. I'm out anyway. I'll see you tomorrow."

"Where are you going?" Jazz asked as she watched Patience quickly zip up her bag and swing it on her shoulders.

"I'm going over to Tyric's house."

Jazz stood and said, "Does Momma know?"

Patience walked out into the hallway and to the family room with Jazz close on her heels. She pulled her keys up out of her pocket and said, "No, she doesn't know, but if she wakes up and asks, let her know."

"How am I supposed to get to school in the morning?"

Patience opened the front door and said, "Ride the bus."

"The bus? You know I'm not getting on the bus."

Once you had a car or rode to school with some-one who owned one it made you seem like a loser if you got demoted back to the bus to get to school.

"I'll play sick and stay home before I get on the bus again."

Patience stepped out on the front porch and said, "I should make you suffer but I won't. I'll swing by and get you in the morning, so be ready."

"Okay," Jazz answered as she locked the door behind her sister and watched her as she climbed inside her car and drove off.

Chapter Thirteen

DeMario tossed Dré the basketball as they played a short game of pickup in Dré's driveway.

"Amigo, I can't believe you kissed Patience. What were you thinking?"

Dré slammed the ball through the hoop and said, "It just happened."

"Denim is pissed! I saw her after school and she wouldn't even stop to talk to me."

Dré walked over to DeMario and said, "Yeah, she's pissed, all right."

"What is wrong with you? After all you and

Denim have gone through, then you go and do something like this?"

He grinned before throwing up a three-point shot.

"DeMario, I have a confession."

He knocked the ball out of Dré's hand and asked, "What kind of confession?"

Before Dré could respond, DeMario answered Dré's three-point shot with one of his own.

"I wanted to kiss Patience."

"That's your confession?" DeMario asked curiously. "Bro, you have lost your mind."

Dré bounced the ball through his legs and said, "Sit down for a second. I need to lay it all out for you and maybe you'll understand why things went down the way that it did."

DeMario reluctantly sat down and listened as Dré explained his sudden interest in Patience. When he was finished, all he could say was, "I'm going to love seeing how you and Denim are going to work this out. I just hope it doesn't backfire on you."

"Me too."

DeMario stood and said, "It's getting late. Good luck with all that you have going on."

"Thanks, bro," Dré replied as he gave DeMario

a brotherly handshake and hug. "We're going to need it."

The next morning, Denim hurried to her class. She was getting sick of the stares and whispers caused by the altercation with Patience. She couldn't wait for school to end so she could finally put all the drama behind her and get on with her life.

"Hey Denim! Wait up!" Kayla yelled.

"What do you want?" Denim asked. "I told you I didn't feel like hanging yesterday."

Kayla ignored her and continued to talk. "Desireé wants to talk to you about Patience."

"She has nothing to say to me that I want to hear. Now for the last time, stay away from me."

Denim walked off but Kayla grabbed her hand, stopping her.

"Are you sure about that? It's not going to be easy going up against Patience alone. We know her better than anyone so we know her weakness. It would be to your advantage to talk to Desireé if you really want to get back at her."

Denim checked the time on her cell phone. "Why do you and Desireé care so much about my beef with Patience? Why the sudden interest in me?"

"I'll let Desireé explain all of that to you. So can I tell her you'll meet?"

She took a step back and said, "I don't know. It sounds kind of fishy to me. I feel like I'm walking into an ambush."

"Do you want to get back at Patience or not?" Kayla asked in a frustrated tone of voice. "Patience had her tongue down your man's throat. Are you going to let her get away with that?"

Denim thought to herself for a minute. She didn't want to seem too anxious but she didn't want the opportunity to get away from her either, so she pointed her finger in Kayla's face and said, "I'll talk to Desireé but I swear if you're trying to set me up, I'll . . ."

Kayla smiled and said, "It's cool, Denim. Nobody's trying to set you up."

"Okay, when and where?"

"Meet us after school at the Market Street Grill. I guarantee you won't be sorry."

Denim turned to walk away and said, "I'll be the judge of that."

As Denim made her way down the hallway, she saw Dré walking in her direction with DeMario. It seemed like everyone else, including Kayla, were anxious to see what was going to happen as they moved closer to each other. Their eyes met and he smiled. Denim tried to turn and go down another hallway but Dré grabbed her arm, preventing her from leaving.

"Turn me loose, Dré."

She was beautiful. Her jeans were fitting her perfectly and her yellow G-Unit T-shirt hugged her womanly curves to perfection.

"Can we talk?" he asked softly.

She pulled her arm out of his grasp and said, "You did all your talking while you were kissing Patience. Stay away from me, prime time."

"Come on, Denim. It didn't mean anything."

Denim stepped up to Dré and said, "It meant everything to me. I trusted you, but not anymore."

"So you're just going to throw away everything we have because of a kiss?" he asked.

DeMario tapped him on the back and said, "Come on, Dré. Leave her alone."

"Hold on, DeMario," he replied angrily as he turned to his best friend. "I'm not through talking to her."

While Dré and DeMario were discussing the situation, Denim stepped around Dré and said, "Goodbye, Dré."

The altercation between Denim and Dré once

again became the topic of conversation around school. They were the prince and princess couple around school but it seemed like their fairy-tale romance had come to end, or did it?

The Market Street Grill was buzzing with activity when Denim arrived. When she walked in, she immediately spotted Kayla and Desireé. They waved her over and Denim reluctantly made her way across the room and slid into the booth.

"You made it," Kayla said with a smile.

"I'm here but I don't know how long I'm going to stay. Why do you want to talk to me?"

Desireé waved the waitress over and said, "Get you something to drink first."

The waitress quickly came over and asked, "What can I get you ladies to drink?"

Denim picked up the menu and said, "A cherry Coke."

Kayla and Desireé gave the waitress their drink orders as well before she walked away. Once the waitress was gone, Desireé said, "I'll make this short and sweet. I heard what Patience did to Dré. I know you're pissed and if you play your cards right we might be in a position to help you take care of her."

"Why do you care about my beef with Patience?" Denim asked.

Desireé leaned forward and whispered, "Because we have something in common. Patience did something that I've been unhappy with for some time now. I just thought we could team up and take care of the problem together."

The waitress placed the drink order down in front of them and then asked, "Are you ladies ready to order?"

Kayla ordered a patty-melt burger and fries. Desireé ordered a catfish sandwich and fries but Denim passed on the food.

"Are you sure you don't want anything?" Desireé asked Denim.

"No, I'm good."

The waitress left to put in Kayla and Desireé's order. Denim took a sip of her drink.

"Hold up. Why would you want to beat down your own? What could she have done so bad for you guys to turn on her? I hear you B.G.R. girls stick together no matter what."

Desireé stared at Denim and wondered if she was doing the right thing by bringing her into their plan. It was a chance she was taking but time was of the essence and she needed to put things to rest once and for all, so she decided to trust her in spite of their previous run-in.

"I'll tell you, but you first have to let me know if you're in or not," Desireé replied.

Denim leaned back in her seat and folded her arms. She was at a crossroad now. Being seen with these girls was risky enough but agreeing to an unknown plan with them was riskier.

"Okay, I'm in," Denim announced. "Now tell me what you're planning to do to Patience and why you have a vendetta against her."

"I guess it's only fair since I know why you're pissed at her but my reason is going to allow us to get paid!"

Hearing that money was involved with their vendetta against Patience shook Denim up a little bit. Who could or would pay them to do something to Patience and why? Worse yet, what had she agreed to? She didn't want to end up in jail. This situation was more sinister than they thought. Now she had to do a lot of maneuvering to get to the truth. The waitress brought their entrées to the table. Kayla and Desireé immediately dug into them.

"What exactly are you planning on doing to Patience?" Denim asked, hoping for a simple answer but something told her it wasn't going to be.

"Kill her, of course," Desireé replied casually. "And it don't come cheap."

Denim's heart thumped hard in her chest. She needed to keep her cool, but it was difficult. Her face had heated up and she could feel sweat beading up on her forehead. She took a sip of her cherry Coke and cleared her throat.

"You're getting paid to kill Patience?"

"What's wrong, Denim? Do you want us to break you off a little change for helping us?" Kayla asked.

"No!" she yelled.

"Are you having second thoughts now since you know what's up?" Desireé asked.

Denim had to answer carefully. She still needed to know why there was a hit on Patience and who ordered it.

"No, I'm not having second thoughts but I would like to know everything before we go any farther."

Kayla said, "We don't have to tell you that in Scotland Heights, there are rules you have to live by. You don't mess with another chick's man, you take care of your own, and you don't snitch. That's not a lot to ask for when you live in the Yard. Patience forgot the rules and now she has to pay."

"So what do you need me for?" Denim asked. "We're not friends anymore, remember?"

Kayla giggled and said, "You're the bait."

Kayla's comment startled Denim. She wasn't trying to be anybody's bait. She was already playing with fire and she had no plans to get burned. Now to find out there was a third party involved raised the stakes.

"Bait? What kind of bait?"

Desireé finished off her sandwich and then pushed her plate to the side.

"All we need you to do is to call Patience and get her to meet you somewhere. Tell her you want to apologize to her for what went down with your man. Once she gets there we'll handle the rest."

"Look, I'm not trying to go to jail for you guys. I mean, I love Dré but he ain't worth all that."

Desireé hit the table with her fist and yelled, "Don't you have any pride? I hate working with you bougie girls! You're involved now and you can't back out."

"Calm down, Desireé," Kayla instructed her. "Denim's looking for justice just like we're trying to get paid."

"I do want justice, but before I make any call, I want to know where the money's coming from. If you guys are going to get paid I might as well get mine too," Denim answered.

The next thing Denim heard was the unfamiliar name, Pit Bull. She didn't know who he was or why he would pay for a hit on Patience but she had a feeling that Patience would know exactly who he was. She didn't want to ask too many questions to make them suspicious, but having the name of the person who ordered the hit was a huge clue. Now she was anxious to get out of the grill so she could regroup. After bidding the two girls good-bye and when she was in the safe confines of her car she frantically sent out a series of text messages. Her hands were shaking and her stomach was in knots. Things were a lot worse than she ever envisioned. A lot worse.

As Desireé drove back to her house, Kayla looked over at her and asked, "Are you sure you're ready to do this? I mean, we're talking about one of our own."

"I just want to get paid," Desireé replied. "This is business, not personal."

"How do you think the other girls are going to act when they find out what we did?" Kayla asked.

"If we do this right, no one has to know we're even involved and if Denim starts running her mouth, we can throw her in for free," she revealed.

"Pit Bull has his reasons for wanting her gone and if he's willing to pay top dollar, I'm willing to take it. If we don't do it he won't have any problem finding somebody else who will."

Later that evening, Tyric sipped on a beer as he watched Patience spoon the barbecue riblets, baked beans and slaw onto their plates. She seemed a little distant and somewhat quieter than normal but he couldn't put his finger on it.

She handed him the plate and said, "Tyric, I need a favor."

He took the plate out of her hands and asked, "What kind of favor?"

"I want you to put a wire on me."

Tyric chuckled. "I can't put a wire on you. What's going on with you today? Your body's here but your mind is somewhere else."

She licked the sauce off her fingers and then looked him in the eyes. She was very independent when it came to handling her personal issues, but this time she needed his help. He'd never denied her anything but to get his help this time she was going to have to reveal some horrific news to him that she knew would send him off the deep end.

Tyric sat the beer bottle down on the table and asked, "Are you in some kind of trouble?"

"Sort of. I found out there's a hit out on me."

"A hit? By who?" he asked angrily.

"Pit Bull," she revealed. "I guess since he's still worried that I'm going snitch on him over the drugs Shawn had in his car. Somehow's he's been able to talk a couple of my B.G.R. girls into carrying it out."

"I've been trying to get that fool locked up for years but every time he's raided, he never has the stash on him," Tyric replied. "He's smart but I'm smarter. There's no way in hell I'm going to let him hurt you."

Tyric stood and picked up his cell phone and punched in a series of numbers.

"Who are you calling?" she asked.

"Don't worry about it. I'm going to have Pit Bull off the streets within the hour."

Patience grabbed the cell phone out of his hand and disconnected the call. "You can't do that. If you do that he'll know I'm on to him. You know we need more evidence and that starts with getting Kayla and Desireé on tape to incriminate him."

"Why am I just hearing about these girls?"

"You know I like to handle my own problems."

"Not where your life is concerned." He picked up a pen and notepad and said, "Give the girls' names."

She took the notepad out of his hand and wrote down Desireé and Kayla's names and slid the notepad back to him.

He tore off the piece of paper and tucked it into his pocket. "How did you find out about the hit?"

"A classmate named Denim Mitchell told me about it. She first overheard them talking about me weeks ago, but at the time I didn't know what they were planning. She only found out it was a hit recently."

"Is this Mitchell girl trustworthy?" Tyric asked.

Patience stood and walked over to the refrigerator and pulled out a Pepsi. Denim had been a great friend to her and she was very trustworthy. She popped open the can and sat back down at the table and said, "Yes, she's very trustworthy."

Tyric studied Patience's body language. He could tell she was unnerved by the information. Pit Bull had been a thorn in her side for a few years now and he knew she carried a lot of guilt over the death of her ex. Tyric had tried everything he could within the letter of the law to take Pit Bull off the streets. Now that he had raised the stakes he would do everything he could to make sure the hit on Patience wasn't carried out and that Pit Bull would be brought to justice and finally be put behind bars where he belonged.

"What about the wire, Tyric?" she asked.

"A wire is not what you need right now."

He left the room and quickly returned with Ryan's gun that he had taken from her weeks before. He sat the gun on the table in front her and said, "Use it if you have to. In the meantime I need to get you out of town until we get Pit Bull and these girls off the streets."

She picked up the gun and said, "Thanks for giving me the gun back, but you can't fight all my battles for me. You know how we do it in Scotland Heights. I have a reputation to uphold and I have to be the one who brings Pit Bull down."

"Scotland Heights, B.G.R., and all this tough-girl stuff is about to be in your past. I'm not going to let you get yourself killed over this."

"Things are already set up," she informed him. "I won't be able to put this matter to rest without you and if things go bad we have to get it on tape."

"I'm going to help you, but we're going to do things my way. No exceptions. Do you understand?"

Patience had to understand that while Tyric did

love her, he was still a police officer and anything he did to help her could affect his career.

She nodded and said, "I understand. Thank you, babe."

"Thank me when Pit Bull is behind bars."

In Langley Heights, Denim had been updating her MySpace page, adding new music and e-mailing Patrice for nearly an hour. It was almost midnight and it was hard for her to act normal, knowing what she knew. The fact was that she wasn't sleepy and knowing she had someone's life in her hands had her stomach in knots. She sent Patrice one last message before turning off her computer. Before climbing into bed she pulled out her diary and recorded a few lines.

Dear Diary,

Things are happening so fast. I found out that what I do over the next few days could mean the difference in life or death for a classmate. I hope I'm doing the right thing and I pray that this will all be over tomorrow.

Later,

D

She closed her diary, climbed into bed, and worried about what tomorrow might bring. As she laid there staring at the way the moon cast shadows on her bedroom walls she willed herself to finally go to sleep.

Chapter Fourteen

"Where have you been?" Jazz asked as she climbed in the passenger side of the car.

"Why are you stressing?" Patience asked as she surveyed her surroundings. She had to be extra-careful now that she knew about the hit. "You've never been in a hurry to get to school before."

She put her seat belt on and said, "I have things to do today. I didn't know you were going to stay over at Tyric's again last night."

"Give me a break, Jazz," she replied as she backed out of the driveway.

"No, you're the one who needs to chill. Just because Momma's okay with you and him hooking up don't mean she approves of you spending the night with him all the time."

"You're right. I really did plan to come home last night but we started watching a movie and I fell asleep. Tyric said he didn't want to wake me."

"TMI!" Jazz yelled out. "Anyway, just so you'll know, I'm giving you a graduation party at the house tonight."

"I don't want a party, Jazz," Patience announced as she sped off toward Langley High School. The last thing she wanted was to have Kayla and Desi-reé in her house acting like everything was cool.

"Well, too bad. You're getting one. I've been planning this for weeks and you're not going to ruin it for me. It's just going to be us and B.G.R."

"It would've been nice if you had asked me, Jazz. I may already have plans."

"Well, you don't and if you do you'll have to break them because this party is going down," Jazz revealed.

"You know I'm trying to distance myself from B.G.R. Why would you plan a party and invite them?"

Patience had stomped on her excitement, hurting her feelings.

"I guess you've forgotten that they've been a big

part of your life over the past five years," she reminded her sister. "You know what, just forget it."

Patience looked over at her sister and saw the sadness in her face. She was right, B.G.R. had been her sisters for the past five years and there had been some good times, but times had changed and it had become harder to trust the ones closest to you. Then again, maybe this was exactly what she needed. Keep your friends close, keep your enemies closer.

"Okay, Jazz! I'll let you give me a party with B.G.R., but this is it and you bet not go overboard."

Jazz clapped her hands in victory and said, "Yes! We're going to have fun. Everybody's so excited about your party."

"What about Momma?" Patience asked.

"Momma's fine. She's going to be next door at Mrs. Brown's house playing bid wiz. Tonight is just for us, but Momma also told me to make sure we keep things tame because your man and his sidekick is going to be stopping by at some point to make sure the girls don't get out of hand."

Patience smiled upon hearing that Tyric would be stopping by. She pulled into the school parking lot and shut off the engine.

"I'll go along with this party of yours on one

condition," Patience announced as she climbed out of the car.

"What condition?" Jazz asked as she grabbed her book bag off the backseat and walked alongside her sister toward school.

"That you announce at the party tonight that this is your last night in B.G.R. because you're moving to Atlanta with me."

Jazz stopped in her tracks.

"Excuse me? I can't go to Atlanta and leave Momma here by herself."

Patience walked over to her sister and smiled. She put her arm around Jazz's neck and said, "You're not going to be leaving Momma alone."

"What are you talking about?"

"Momma has a boyfriend."

"A boyfriend? How do you know?" Jazz asked with a snarl on her face.

"I saw Momma and a man named Barrington kissing in the park one night so I jotted down the license plate and had Tyric run a background check on him."

Jazz was stunned. First Patience announces she's dating Tyric, now she finds out that her mother has a man. What next?

"Why hasn't Momma told us about him?"

"I don't know," Patience answered. "You know she hasn't dated anybody since Daddy died."

The sisters entered the school and walked down the hallway.

"What did Tyric find out about him?" Jazz asked.

"He lives over in Piedmont and he's a bank manager. He's got two kids in college and he's divorced. From what Tyric said, he seems to be a cool guy."

Patience followed Jazz over to her locker. She opened it, pulled out her history book and then closed it.

"So, are you going to ask Momma about her boyfriend?" Jazz asked.

"Not yet. I have some other things on my mind right now, but I will if she don't tell us about him by the time *we* get ready to leave for Atlanta."

Minutes later, Denim abruptly interrupted them in the hallway.

"Hey, Jazz. I need to talk to Patience. It's kind of important. Can you give us a second?"

Jazz studied Denim to make sure she wasn't going to be hostile with Patience. Their last encounter ended in violence and even though she knew Patience could handle Denim, she still had her back. "Are you cool, sis?"

"I'm good. I'll see you after school."

Jazz made her way around the corner, leaving Patience and Denim alone. Denim and Patience noticed they had an audience who immediately started whispering when they saw the two of them talking. Since their previous altercation, everyone had been watching and waiting to see if anything else was going to jump off between them because of the now infamous kiss with Dré.

"What's up, Mitchell?" Patience asked as they continued to walk through the crowded hallway.

Denim proceeded to talk to Patience about everything that had taken place between them over the past few weeks as well as the most recent events. They'd had their highs and lows and now that things were coming to a quick end, Denim wanted their relationship to end on a high note. Classmates watched from near and far, some hoping for a second catfight between the two attractive young women, especially the guys. Unfortunately, their hopes were quickly diminished as the girls continued to make their way to class.

"Is everything cool between you and Dré?" Patience asked.

"I still can't believe he kissed you like that."

"Don't be so hard on him," Patience suggested. "He loves you."

"I know," Denim replied softly.

Patience noticed Dré and DeMario walking down the hallway in their direction. She nodded in their direction and said, "Dré would never mess around on you, Mitchell. He's a good catch. Make sure you hold onto him."

"I'll will," she answered. "Listen, Patience, are you going to be okay?"

"Yeah, I'm good."

Denim touched her arm and said, "You are being careful, right?"

"As much as possible," she answered. "Look, Denim, I have to run. I'll see you later."

Denim bumped her fist against Patience before she walked off. Seconds later she got a text message on her cell phone. She pulled it out of her book bag and read the message.

Thanks for everything. If I never get a chance to tell you, you've been a great friend and I'll never forget you.
Patience

Denim closed her phone and watched as Dré made his way through the crowd of students. Denim felt her body heat up as he got closer to her. She could see the love in his eyes as he backed her into the lockers and planted a firm kiss on her lips right in front of everyone. The kiss they shared left little question to whether the couple was still together. DeMario cleared his throat to get the couple's attention. The principal, Mr. McLemore, was walking in their direction and as he made his way down the hallway, he chastised students for violating the dress code, running in the hallway, and for being late to class, which is exactly what Denim and Dré were doing.

"Nice save, DeMario. I guess I'd better get to class before he gets to us," Denim announced.

Dré quickly kissed her on the lips and said, "I'll see you later."

All three quickly hurried off to class before Mr. McLemore finished inspecting the hallways.

V-Chip looked over at Tyric and asked, "Are you serious?"

"Yeah, I'm serious."

V-Chip shook his head and picked up a piece of

the electronic equipment and closely inspected it. He couldn't believe that Pit Bull had been stupid enough to order a hit on Tyric's girl.

"Bro, what is that punk thinking? You know we have to take him down quick, right?"

"If it was up to me, he would already be over at the morgue."

"You know that can be arranged very discreetly if you're serious," V-Chip replied with a sly grin on his face.

"Don't think I haven't already thought about it. If something happens to my baby I don't know what I'm going to do."

"From what you've told me, Brianna will be fine. Don't worry. I got your back," V-Chip reminded him.

V-Chip studied Tyric's body language. He'd seen him angry before but talking about Brianna getting hurt or worse really set him off. Only a man truly in love would react like that. He picked up the piece of equipment that Tyric previously held and adjusted it.

"You know what, Tyric?"

"What?" Tyric asked as he looked out the passenger-side window.

"I'm glad you're with Brianna and even though

she's a lot younger than the other women who be sweating you, she's cool."

Tyric looked over at his partner and asked, "You mean that?"

"Of course I do. I'm glad you found someone who's just as wild about you as you are over them."

"I appreciate that," Tyric replied as he held his hand out for V-Chip.

V-Chip grabbed Tyric's hand and then gave him a high five before continuing to work on the electronic equipment. He often teased Tyric about Brianna's age but the fact was that it wasn't up to him.

V-Chip turned on the CD player and bounced his head to a Raheem DeVaughn song.

"So when is this wiring ceremony going to take place?" V-Chip asked.

"I got a text from Brianna earlier saying she wanted to do it tonight. Jazz is having a B.G.R. graduation party for her at their house."

"Selena okayed that?" V-Chip asked.

"Yeah, but she's going to be next door playing cards. She asked if we would run through and look in on them, so we might as well do it then."

V-Chip put the electronic device back into an inconspicuous case and said, "I'm down for whatever, Tyric. You know I don't mine helping your girl."

"Thanks, bro."

Tyric put his seat belt on as V-Chip pulled out into traffic.

Jazz hurried around the house making sure everything was in place for the graduation party.

"Patience!" she yelled. "Where does Momma keep the large utensils?"

Patience walked into the kitchen and casually opened a cabinet drawer.

"Where did you get all this food?"

Jazz had cheese and crackers, hot wings, chips, chicken salad sandwiches, and pasta salad.

"Momma bought the cake, drinks, and paper products, but I bought the rest."

"That's cool, Jazz."

"Thanks, now, are you going to give me a hand? I'm having a little trouble finding stuff in here."

"If you spent more time in the kitchen you would know where everything was."

"If you're going to help me, Patience, help me. Don't dog me," Jazz replied as she arranged the utensils on the table.

With her hands on her hips, Patience said, "Why

should I have to help you? I thought I was the guest of honor?"

"You know I'm unorganized and I want everything to be nice. You're better at this than I am."

Patience picked up a piece of cheese and popped it into her mouth.

"Sorry Charlie, no can do. I love you, Jazz, but I'm not trying to be a caterer tonight."

Jazz rolled her eyes as she watched Patience grab a handful of chips.

"Well, you look nice whether you help me or not."

Patience twirled around as if she was modeling. She was sporting a pair of designer blue jeans, two-inch red sandals, and a red halter top.

"Why, thank you, Jazz."

"Red is your color, Patience. Well, any color looks good on you. Your skin color is so pretty."

Patience picked up a napkin and wiped the corner of her mouth and smiled.

"Wow, Jazz, you're going to give me the big head if you keep that up."

Jazz put the tray of hot wings on the table and said, "You know you're gorgeous. I wish I looked like you."

"You do look like me! I'm just taller and your

hair is shorter and a lighter auburn color than mine."

Jazz knew she was attractive but Patience was always the one who got all the attention from guys. She knew her height had a lot to do with it, but she couldn't ignore the fact that she was beautiful and since they did share a resemblance, it meant she was beautiful as well.

"Jazz, before everyone get here I need to talk to you about a few things."

She looked over at Patience as she uncovered the graduation cake. "Sounds serious, what's up?"

"You'd better sit down for this one and please don't freak out."

"Don't freak out? Why would I freak out? Are you pregnant?"

"No! I'm not pregnant, fool," Patience replied as they sat down on the sofa.

Jazz put her hand over her heart and said, "Whew! I'm glad, because Momma would kill you if you were."

Patience waved Jazz off and asked, "How well do you know Kayla and Desireé?"

She thought to herself and then said, "About as well as you do. Remember they came to us wanting to join up last year. Why?"

Patience began to tell Jazz everything that had taken place, beginning with Denim overhearing their conversation in the deli all the way up to what she had planned for tonight.

Jazz was completely stunned. She stood and paced the floor as the information Patience told her sunk in. Why would some of the sisters in B.G.R. want to hurt her?

"Wait a minute. You mean to tell me that those heifers have been plotting something against you all this time?"

"Money talks," Patience reminded her.

Tears welled up in Jazz's eyes, not because she was sad but because she was angry.

"I can't believe that two of our own would be capable of doing something like this. So you and Denim are not really feuding over Dré?"

"No, we're not. It was a plan just so Denim could get close to them and they would let their guard down so she could find out more information."

"What about Mercedes? Is she involved too?" Jazz asked.

"I don't think so. I haven't seen her hanging out with them in a while."

"Sis, you should've told me a long time ago."

Patience reluctantly revealed to Jazz how Pit

Bull threatened to hurt her and their mother if she ever told anyone about the drugs. She had always been a liability to him and it was safer for his business if she was out of the way.

Jazz waved her hands in the air and yelled, "The party's off! I don't want any of them in this house!"

"You can't do that, Jazz. Tyric is going to help me end this tonight one way or the other."

Jazz walked over to the front door and stared out into the night.

"Okay, I'm in. Just tell me what you need me to do."

Chapter Fifteen

The party had been going great in spite of the knowledge Patience and Jazz had on Kayla and Desireé. It was difficult for the sisters to party with their friends but they did the best they could to act normal. Jazz had the music blasting as they danced happily together. Patience hugged each one as they presented her with gifts for her upcoming graduation. She received bath products, gift cards, jewelry, and other nice offerings of affection. It was a joyous time but on more than one occasion she had to stop Jazz from glaring at Desireé and Kayla.

The night was still young when V-Chip and Tyric walked through the door and surveyed the crowd.

Tyric and Patience's faces lit up as their eyes immediately connected. Patience had texted him earlier to let him know that she had told Jazz everything and to Tyric their safety meant everything to him.

"Showtime," Jazz mumbled as she walked from the kitchen into the living room to greet them.

"What are you doing here?" she joked with Tyric as he grabbed a hot wing and put it up to his mouth.

He gave her a kiss on the cheek and jokingly said, "I'm here because I can be. Who told you you could have a party anyway?"

"My momma did and I don't think you're Selena Baxter," she joked back.

All the girls laughed at their exchange. They all knew of Tyric's close relationship with the Baxter family after Ryan's death, but they didn't know that Patience was dating him.

"What's up, you squares?" V-Chip yelled out.

Jazz walked over to V-Chip and blocked him from getting to the table where the food was laid out.

"Tyric! Please don't you let your boy eat up all the food."

V-Chip pulled out a twenty-dollar bill and slapped it in Jazz's hand.

"Here you go, slim. Now make me a plate," he teased as he sat on the sofa between a couple of the girls and started casually talking to them.

"I'm not making you a plate, but I will keep the twenty. You're welcome to the food but please try and leave some for our guests," Jazz replied.

Tyric walked over to Patience and gave her a loving hug.

"You look unbelievable," he whispered into her ear. "You'd better be glad you have a house full of people. Otherwise I might have to—"

She blushed and said, "Be quiet, Tyric. Come on in the bedroom and wire me with your nasty self."

He chuckled.

"What will people think about us being alone in the bedroom, Miss Baxter" he asked with a mischievous grin on his face.

"Behave, Tyric, but you are right. That might cause a problem," she answered in agreement. "Oh! I got it. You can help me move my gifts into the bedroom."

"That will work," he replied as he followed Patience across the room to the area where all her gifts were laid out and helped her transport them to her bedroom.

* * *

Across town in Langley Heights, Denim pulled into Dré's driveway and put the car in park. She picked up her cell phone and dialed his number and waited for him to answer.

"I'm outside, Dré, are you ready to go?"

"I'll be right out, babe."

Denim hung up and then sent Patience a text. Almost immediately, she received a reply. They were meeting in thirty minutes and her heartbeat was starting to speed up.

Dré climbed into the passenger seat and immediately leaned over and gave her a kiss on the lips.

"Dang, you smell good. Is everything still on for tonight?"

She put the car in reverse and said, "Yeah. I just called Patience. I'm starting to get nervous, Dré."

He looked through her CDs and found a mixed CD of various hip-hop artists. He slid it into her CD player and said, "You know you don't have to go through with this. Just say the word and we can just hang out here or at your house and let Patience settle this by herself."

For a split second Denim thought about it, but she'd given her word and she couldn't turn back now. She was too important to the entire plan and if she didn't show up, there was no telling what might happen.

"I gave my word, Dré," she replied. "Do you have the camera?"

"Right here," he responded as he patted his jacket pocket.

"Good, let's do this," she said as she drove down the dark street toward the park.

After Tyric discreetly attached the wire to Patience's body, they exited the bedroom and rejoined the group. She had received the call from Denim while she was in the bedroom, requesting a meeting in the city park.

"Hey guys, I hate to run out on my party, but I have a very important errand to run," Patience announced as she grabbed her keys and walked toward the front door. "Feel free to hang out here a little while longer and enjoy the music and food. This shouldn't take long."

She exited the house and seconds later, V-Chip and Tyric also exited but not before having a private conversation with Jazz.

Within minutes, Kayla and Desireé received text messages from Denim letting them know that she had made the call they wanted her to. Minutes later the pair suddenly decided to call it a night, causing Jazz to go ahead and end the party. Events were put in motion that could possibly cause an explosive end to what started as a joyous night.

Patience pulled into the city park and made her way over to the playground area. She had arrived before Denim so she parked and slowly exited her car. The park could be scary at night but for Patience it was peaceful. She sat in one of the swings and waited for Denim.

Seconds later she noticed the headlights of a car pulling in next to hers. She stood and waited as the female figure approached her. When she finally made her way into the light, Patience realized it wasn't Denim, but Desireé.

Patience's heart skipped a beat, but she couldn't show fear as she stood and slid her hands inside her jacket pockets.

"What are you doing here? I was supposed to meet Denim."

She walked closer to Patience and said, "Oh, don't worry, Denim will be here shortly. Aren't you happy to see me?"

Patience carefully scanned the area and noticed that Desireé had one hand behind her back.

"What do you want, Desireé?"

"What I want, Patience, is to get paid and you are my meal ticket."

Patience frowned and said, "You're talking crazy. I'm nobody's meal ticket."

Desireé turned and looked over her shoulder as Kayla and Denim made their way over to the playground.

"Denim?" Patience called out to her. "What are you doing here with these losers?"

"I'm sorry, Patience. I didn't want things between us to be like this but you forced my hand when you kissed my man."

"Shut up, Denim! As matter of fact, you can leave. I don't need you anymore," Desireé yelled as she pulled a small handgun from behind her back.

Patience gritted her teeth and said, "Now I know you're crazy. I can't believe you would pull a gun on me. Why are you doing this?"

"Pit Bull said you would be clueless."

"So you're doing this because Pit Bull told you to?" Patience asked.

"He has deep pockets and I sick of being poor so

I jumped on the chance when he offered me a couple of grand to take you out. Sorry, Patience, this is business," Desireé explained.

"Desireé, you can't do this," Denim called out to her. "A person's life is worth more than two thousand dollars."

"Didn't I tell you to leave or do you want some of this too?" Desireé yelled as she aimed the gun briefly in Denim's direction.

Kayla stepped up and said, "Chill, Desireé. This is not about Denim. Hurry up and do this so we can get out of here."

"Shut up, Kayla," Desireé yelled. "And while we're at it, I hope you don't think I'm going to share Pit Bull's payoff with you."

"What are you saying, Desireé?" Kayla asked.

"I'm saying I don't need you either. After I do this, Pit Bull said he could help me make all kinds of money. The sky is the limit and from where I'm standing, that don't include you."

This was the information Patience was looking for and it startled her but she had to remain composed since Desireé was so emotional. Her hands were shaking and the slightest twitch could make her pull the trigger with a tragic result.

"Put the gun down," Tyric yelled at Desireé as he and V-Chip stepped out of a row of nearby trees.

V-Chip grabbed Kayla by the arm, put handcuffs on her, sat her down on the ground, and quickly urged Denim to move out of the line of fire.

"You set me up?" Desireé asked as she looked angrily at Patience.

"You set yourself up," Patience replied. "Put the gun down, Desireé. It's over. The police have everything you said about Pit Bull on tape."

Tyric moved around in front of Patience and yelled once again for Desireé to put her gun down but she still aimed it in Patience's direction.

"How did you know we were going to be here?" Desireé curiously asked Patience.

"It was me," Denim admitted as she walked back over to the area. "I overheard you guys talking about setting Patience up one day in Martelli's deli. I didn't know what you were planning at the time but I still had to warn her and I'm glad I did."

Patience stared at Desireé and said, "You're stupid, Desireé, if you think Pit Bull is going to do anything for you except use you. He only looks out for himself and I know that from personal experience."

Desireé looked at Denim, Patience, and lastly at Tyric. She slowly started to raise the gun toward her head but Tyric shot the gun out of her hand, preventing her from harming herself. V-Chip quickly handcuffed her while Tyric turned to Patience and pulled her into his arms.

"Are you okay, Brianna?"

"Yeah, I'm good," she replied as she pulled the electronic device out of her top and handed it to him.

Dré moved toward the group and held a small camcorder. He looked at Denim and said, "I nearly lost it when she pointed that gun at you."

"You're not by yourself," she replied as she hugged his neck. "Did you get everything?"

"Yeah, I got it loud and clear."

It had been an eventful night and now all Patience wanted to do was go home, take a hot bath, and go to bed in the arms of Tyric. At nearly the same time, officers raided two of Pit Bull's houses simultaneously, hitting the mother lode of guns, drugs, and thousands of dollars—enough evidence along that would lock him up for life. With the help of the audiotape and Dré's video, Tyric had an airtight case against him for conspiracy to commit murder.

* * *

Later that night, Denim looked in the mirror and realized just how bad things could've gone tonight but through the grace of God, everyone was safe and sound. She was somewhat saddened that Desireé had let a ruthless thug like Pit Bull convince her to commit a heinous crime all for the sake of the almighty dollar. Hopefully she would get the help she needed to get her life back on track.

Denim was eternally grateful that God had put her at the right place at the right time in order to overhear portions of a conversation that would turn out to be a sinister plan against a fellow classmate. Yes, they came from different worlds but they weren't that different after all. Denim had saved another person's life and it felt good. What she witnessed tonight was terrifying and sad and she never wanted to be involved in a situation like that ever again.

As she sat down on the side of her bed and held her head in her hands, she thought about her blessed life with great parents and dear friends and it hit home with her that everyone was not as fortunate. Before going to bed, she did what she often did. She pulled out her diary and began to jot down her thoughts.

Dear Diary,

Tonight was a night full of sadness and terror. With several people's help we were able to set things up so Patience could put the people who wanted to harm her behind bars. It was actually deeper than any of us ever imagined. It involved drugs, money, and murder with a sad ending for Desireé. She's okay physically but she might be looking at some serious jail time for her part in the scheme. Now Patience can go on to college with a clear conscience and a light heart. Daddy always tells me that everything happens for a reason and now I believe him more than ever. I'm glad Patience and I are friends and while I'm going to miss her when she leaves for Spelman, I'm looking forward to seeing her graduation. It's late and I hope sleep comes to me easy tonight.

Until next time.

D.

Chapter Sixteen

"Brianna Baxter," Principal McLemore called out as everyone watched Patience walk across the stage to get her gold cords for graduating with honors and her diploma. The entire family clapped with excitement as did Tyric, V-Chip, Denim, and Dré.

Jazz leaned over to Tyric and whispered, "She looks beautiful, doesn't she?"

Tyric nodded in agreement. "She sure does," he mumbled to himself. "She sure does."

After graduation, Selena gave her daughter an official graduation party. It was a beautiful and warm day, which allowed Selena to have the party outside in the backyard. All their family and friends were there, even Denim, Dré, DeMario, and Patrice. Another surprise guest was Selena's mysterious boyfriend, Barrington Miller.

"Brianna, aren't you going to introduce me to your friends?" Selena asked.

"Yes, Momma, this is DeMario, Patrice, and Dré." She put her arm around Denim's neck and said, "And this is my good friend Denim Mitchell. I wouldn't have made it to this day without her."

Selena hugged each and every one of them but she hugged Denim just a little tighter.

"Denim, I'm so glad my girls have such good friends. You're welcome here any time."

"Thank you, Mrs. Baxter."

Patience waved Jazz over and said, "Okay, Momma, who's the tall, dark, handsome man?"

"Oh, that's just a friend of mine named, Barrington Miller."

"A friend, huh?" Patience asked. "What kind of friend?"

"Okay! Okay! I've been dating him for a few months," she answered with a smile as she looked across the room at him.

"Why didn't you tell us about him, Momma?" Jazz asked.

"The same reason Brianna was afraid to tell us

about Tyric," she admitted. "You two have to understand, I haven't brought a man around you since your father passed away. I don't take that lightly and before I bring someone around I have to know he's respectable and it's something with the possibility of being long-term and not just a fling."

"A fling?" Jazz asked. "Momma, you're not supposed to have a fling."

They all laughed together.

"I know. That's why I invited him here tonight. He's a wonderful man," Selena revealed. "And I want you to meet him."

Selena waved Barrington over and introduced him to her daughters. From that moment, Jazz and Patience both could tell he was highly educated and a true gentleman. They could see why their mother was so smitten with him.

Tyric walked over and joined the Baxter women and Barrington. He took a sip of punch before Selena introduced him to Barrington.

"It's nice to meet you, sir."

"Likewise, Tyric, but please call me Barry. Hearing someone call me sir makes me feel old," he revealed.

"Consider it done," Tyric replied as he shook Barrington's hand. "May I borrow Selena for a second?"

"Go right ahead, young man," Barrington answered.

"Selena, may I talk to you for a second?" Tyric asked.

She followed Tyric off to the side so they could talk privately. While they talked, Denim made her way over to Patience and congratulated her once again.

"Well, Patience, it seems like you're out of here. Who knows, I might join you at Spelman after I graduate."

"I'd like that, Denim," she happily answered.

Just then, Tyric called everyone's attention for some type of announcement.

"May I have your attention, please?" he asked.

Patience and everyone else turned their attention to him.

"As some of you may or may not know, I've been a part of the Baxter family for some time now. I was blessed to meet Ryan, who eventually became like a brother to me. I love him and I miss him dearly. He was a great police officer and a dear friend. When Ryan was called up for a higher duty in heaven, I felt like it was my job to step in and look over Selena, Jasmine, and Brianna. I have no doubt that Ryan is here with us today to help us celebrate Brianna's graduation."

Patience was emotionally touched by Tyric's speech and continued to listen to him along with everyone else as he made his way over to her and took her hands into his.

"I love you, Brianna, and I want the world to know," he proclaimed to her as he dropped down on one knee.

Slightly embarrassed, Patience asked, "What are you doing?"

"Brianna, you're the only woman for me and nothing would make me happier than to have you by my side for the rest of my life. Will you marry me?"

All you could hear were gasps from all the family and guests.

"Married?" Jazz said aloud. "How is Patience going to get married if she's going to college?"

Selena looked over at her youngest daughter and instructed her to be quiet.

Tyric pulled a small, white velvet box out of his pocket, opened it and revealed a marquise diamond solitaire to Patience.

"Brianna? Will you marry me?" he asked again.

Patience was speechless as she allowed Tyric to

slide the ring onto her finger. Tears flowed out of her eyes as she tried to speak.

He stood and cupped her face and said, "I love you."

"I love you too, Tyric, but how can I marry you when I'll be in Georgia and you'll be here?"

Tyric kissed her softly on the lips and said, "Because I'm moving to Atlanta with you, baby. I was able to get a job on the vice squad in Atlanta so you have nothing to worry about."

"I don't know what to say, Tyric."

"How about . . . yes?"

Patience nodded and threw her arms around his neck and said, "Yes! Yes,! Yes, baby, I'll marry you."

The entire yard full of people burst out in applause and you could even hear a few sniffles among the crowd as well.

Patience's grandmother held up her glass of champagne and said, "See, that's how you do it. My second husband, Gilbert, proposed to me like that. He was a gentleman. It's good to see that some of these young men are still gentleman."

"I'll drink to that," Aunt Gracie responded.

"Now that was smooth," Dré pointed out as he walked over and kissed Denim on the cheek. "That's how I'm going to do it when I get ready to propose."

Denim put her hand on her hip and said, "Is that so, prime time?"

He hugged her small waist and said, "Without a doubt."

The young couple shared a series of kisses before Denim suddenly pulled away and looked at her watch.

"Oh my God! I have to get to work."

"Work? I thought you were off today." Dré asked.

"I am basically, but they asked me to come by to show a new intern around the clinic today."

"I was hoping we would get to hang out the rest of the day."

She grabbed her purse and kissed him again on the lips.

"I know, baby, but this student is new. I know how it feels to be the new kid on the block. I shouldn't be long. Do you want to wait for me here or do you want me to come by your house when I'm done?" she asked.

"You can come by the house," he replied. "Come on, I'll walk you out."

Denim said her good-byes to Patience and her family and all the rest of the guests before walking out the door.

*   *   *

At the clinic, Denim hurried into the building to meet the new intern. When she walked into the office she came face-to-face with sixteen-year-old Levar Ray, a sophomore at their rival high school, Piedmont High. He stood when Denim walked into the office. He was cute and stood about three inches shorter than Dré. He was also a lighter complexion than Dré but he was well groomed and was very muscular.

Her supervisor, Tony, stood and said, "Denim, I'd like you to meet Levar Ray. Levar, this is Denim Mitchell, a very talented and future successful physical therapist."

Denim held her hand out and said, "Nice to meet you, Levar."

He blushed and said, "Nice to meet you too, Denim."

"So are you ready for your tour?" Denim asked.

He shoved his hands into his pockets and said, "Whenever you are. Lead the way."

Denim gave him a tour of the clinic as well as sharing with him how fulfilling the intern program had been for her. Levar seemed mesmerized and hung on her every word.

At the end of the tour Denim turned to him and

said, "Well, that about does it. I'm sure you'll like it here."

"So are you going to work here through the summer?" Levar asked.

"You bet. I have somewhat of a shopping fetish," she revealed. "Seriously, though, I love working here, the money's good and it fits in with my school schedule perfectly," she said.

Levar held his hand to shake Denim's hand.

"Sounds good. Thanks for showing me around. I guess I'll see you on Monday."

"I'm off on Monday, so I'll see you Tuesday," Denim replied as she shook his hand. "Have a great weekend."

He slowly released her hand and said, "You too, Denim. Good-bye."

Levar stood and watched as Denim made her way out the door and onto the elevator. The few hours they had spent together put him at ease and while he tried his best to pay attention to what she was saying, he couldn't take his eyes off her beautiful face and her slamming body.

Epilogue

One month later, Tyric and Patience exchanged vows in a small ceremony at Selena's church. Jasmine and Denim stood by her side as her bridesmaids in their lovely red chiffon spaghetti-strapped, tea-length dresses. V-Chip and Tyric's brother stood in support of Tyric, who looked handsome in his tuxedo. His groomsmen also wore black tuxedos but with red neckties to match the bridesmaid dresses. Patience made a beautiful bride in her long, white allover beaded lace wedding dress, which included an illusion halter neckline with a red sash to match the bridesmaid dresses and a chapel train. She wore her hair in a neat updo with cascading curls. She was breathtaking and on that special day she decided it was time for her to drop the nickname that she'd carried with her since she was fourteen and a member of B.G.R. She was anxious to get back to using her legal name, Brianna, again since it was the beginning of a new life and big dreams with Tyric.

The reception was intimate with family and close friends, which consisted of a sit-down dinner and a three-tier wedding cake with white butter cream icing beautifully decorated with red edible roses made from sugar, topped off with a large bouquet of roses on the top tier. As Brianna and Tyric cut the cake she realized that in spite of tragedy and heartache, life goes on. She was happy beyond her wildest imagination and so was her mother with Barrington Miller and Jasmine with her new appreciation for the value of a good education.

The young newlyweds were looking forward to their new lives in Atlanta, Tyric on his new job and Brianna's first day as a freshman at Spelman. Through it all, Brianna learned that with hard work, a strong faith, and good friends, the sky was the limit.

Later that evening, Denim opened her diary and began to write.

Dear Diary,

Today I was a bridesmaid in Brianna's wedding and she was beautiful and happy. It was a very emotional ceremony, not only for the bride and groom but for the families as well. Brianna is a success story from Scotland Heights and I have no doubt that she's going to be an excellent student at Spelman and a great wife to her new husband. So many kids in Scotland Heights have the potential to be and do great things with their lives. They just have to tap into those gifts and make them become a reality just like De-Mario and Brianna did.

Until next time . . .

D